One determined Homicide Detective is good at puzzles. That is how he sees each crime as a puzzle to be solved. But this time, he has his work cut out for him. In the puzzle, there is his connection to BDSM life; there are three quick murders, and then he adds more pieces. There are some wealthy widows who have a connection to a special sex club, and so much time is spent chasing down many more leads.

Until a large tragedy strikes home, this angry detective sets out to solve all the puzzles and take down the killer.

The Mask of Puzzles
Copyright © 2024 M. Garnet
ISBN: 978-1-4874-4239-2
Cover art by SudaGraphics Inc

Published by eXtasy Books Inc

Look for us online at:
www.eXtasybooks.com

THE MASK OF PUZZLES

BY

M. GARNET

ACKNOWLEDGMENTS

I also need to acknowledge the great work by SudaGraphics, Inc. for the distinctive covers that she designs for each of my stories. Covers DO help sell books.

CHAPTER ONE

The sex club was called La Masque, and in the rain of the night, the reflection of the lights from all of the police cars seemed out of place.

The street police, in their raincoats and plastic wraps on their caps, looked up and then stepped back to allow the tall man in the dark, long leather coat to move through. It was the gold badge that marked him as a detective and gave him the right to go past the crime scene. Following him closely was a short female who wore a similar gold badge and must have been his partner. She was trying to keep the raindrops off her pad as she read something on the screen.

They both stopped under the long awning and took time to put the blue booties on their wet shoes. Standing, the tall guy pulled out some thin blue rubber gloves and pulled one on, holding the other in his hand. He nodded at the cop at the door and let the man hold the door open for them.

Stepping into the surreal reception room, they were into an area that would have cost most people ten thousand dollars to stand in this red velvet room with the candles and pale light.

"Let's get the lights turned on everywhere."

The scene did have a different appearance in the bright white lights. Yet, as they looked around, their first surprise was how clean everything was in this red-paneled room. A policeman stood there with a young man who was dressed in a strange outfit. There was a body of a man on the floor, still dressed as a customer at any good restaurant. He was dead

1

with a large hole in his head.

The cop spoke first. "I'm patrolman Mosco. I guess you two are the detectives in charge?"

The tall man nodded. "I'm Detective Reed Bower, this is my partner Detective Roberta Pervis. Where are the scenes of the homicides?"

Patrolman Mosco turned and motioned to the young man in the strange costume. It was a pair of really tight pants that outlined everything, including his genitals. The pants were red and fitted low on his hips. He also had on a red vest that had only one button that was cut out to show each of his nipples. He was holding a mask in one hand.

Mosco smiled as he introduced the man. "This is Charlie, who works here. He was in the storage room and has been cleared. The owner has assigned him to escort you through the club."

Detective Rob raised her pad and took a picture of Charlie and Patrolman Mosco. Deciding to wait and see the other two bodies, Reed didn't do much more than see the dead body had been turned over. It was Reed who gave the instructions, crisp and expected to be obeyed.

"Thanks, Patrolman. Stay here for now. Charlie, let's go to the first site. We have been notified that three bodies were found here tonight, correct?" Reed looked at Charlie with the last word.

Charlie looked down and stepped forward, in an action that all three of the police found strange.

Then Reed nodded as he had been in kink situations before. Charlie had accepted him as a Dom, interesting. "Charlie, no role-playing now. This is real life. Lead us to the murder sites." Reed spoke in a harsh voice, hoping to break through the youth's natural submissive nature.

"Yes, this way M . . . "

"Stop," Reed ordered. "Call me Detective." He knew the

kid was about to call him Master. Damn, he hated these sex clubs.

"Yes, Detective. Please come this way." The young man led them past the curved reception desk and down a long hall. The lights here were almost too bright to reflect the polished wood on the walls and the deep red carpeting.

"What did the original report say, Rob?" Reed asked of his partner.

Rob did some taps on her large pad as she walked with her head tilted to read. "Police called at twelve oh five am that a body had been found. Police reported that upon arriving at the location, there were a lot of people leaving the scene. They called for backup and started to hold people outside the address."

"By twelve forty two, with additional officers on the scene, many adults were being held in the backs of official vehicles, and the first officers entered the site to discover more than one deceased adult in separate areas of the address. The final report of three adults dead under unusual conditions and all adults that had been detained were questioned. All officers and adults left the scene to wait for detectives, coroner, and forensic team."

By this time, they were at the end of the hall, and in the first room was a bar and several tables. Rob thought it looked like any standard fancy place in town until she saw the first set of handcuffs and chains. "What the hell?" Needless to say, even though she had been on the police department for some time, this was her first introduction to a BDSM club.

"Hey, Reed. This club has been open for a couple of years, but there has not been a cop call for it in all that time."

Nodding as he listened to Rob, Reed did his usual quick

glance and took in small details that most would have missed. There was a half-finished drink on the bar. There was only one shoe, a woman's, under one table. Most of the handcuffs were closed, but he did see a couple that were open. One chair was turned over. All the furniture in this room was heavy and expensive. The customers here would be comfortable.

"People left this room in a hurry," Reed mumbled, and Rob made a note on her pad. "Did the house give a *safe* word when the first body was found?"

They were walking through the room, heading for a large exit that led to another area. Reed addressed his question to Charlie.

"No, Detective. Not until later."

As they moved into the next long room, the lights in here seemed to be an insult. Rob moved closer to her partner and tapped him with her pad. "Safe word?"

Stopping, he looked down at the small woman and knew she could take anything that was thrown at her. This world of BDSM might be new to her, but he had worked with her for enough time to know she had the backbone to handle anything.

"Everyone has a safe word that means stop. A club like this also has a master safe word that it probably hopes it never has to use, to ask everyone to stop immediately what they are doing."

Now they went ahead and entered the place where the unusual but interesting activity took place in this sex club. All the hidden ceiling lights revealed what Rob obviously thought looked like a torture chamber.

One dead man was hanging on a standard X platform, tied in soft cotton ropes at arms and heels. But usually, the sub would be smiling at his Master. This one's head was down, and there was a bloody hole in the chest. Below, stretched out in her pool of blood, was a naked young woman holding a small gun in one hand.

Pulling on the second tight, thin blue glove, Bower went down on a heel next to the girl, looking at the gun and the bloody mess in her shoulder. Reed had played this game for a long time and still hated the rules. He swallowed to keep his stomach calm, after all, it wouldn't look good to the guys in blue for a gold shield to throw up. No, he smiled to himself as he thought of what it took to reach this position and how he hated all of it.

This was the Homicide Division, and inside, the tall, handsome detective with the gold shield was all bluff. He knew he was in the business of stopping the bad guys, but why couldn't he stop them before they produced these types of scenes?

This was what he was and what he did as he looked at the red spreading across the floor, reminding him of the time he dropped the full V-8 juice on the kitchen tile. Red on white was never appealing, but for a pretty young woman, it was just wrong.

Being careful not to move anything, he checked the neck of the girl, knowing she was dead, but to see if she was cold. There was still some warmth to her skin through the thin gloves on his fingers. This close, he got a good look at the small weapon in her hand.

"So, she killed him?" It was Rob who was standing back and taking photos with her big tablet.

Without looking over his shoulder, he continued to look at the area, letting his mind search for anything that was out of place. "Not with this small twenty-two."

Staring across the body, Bower finally saw what he was looking for, and the chairs had been moved out of the way. Not as if patrons had jumped up to run for the front exit. No, several pushed away in the same direction as someone was making their way out toward the back. Someone who had put the big holes, one each, in these two people.

"Reed, Forensics is here and is asking to come inside." Rob, as usual, had full attention to the guys in blue and the rest of the team. She was good at her job, which was as his partner, and did not ask him too many personal questions. She was married with one kid, so she never flirted with him like the other women in the precinct.

They had been together for only three months, but Bower had decided it was a permanent arrangement. His last partner had been shot and was on assigned desk duty due to a spine injury.

"Let them in. I want their opinion on the caliber of the weapon." Getting up, Bower carefully moved around the body to follow the path of moved chairs.

From his experience in such clubs, the chairs and any place for the Dom were very comfortable, so these chairs had deep cushions and padded backs. On the other hand, where the subs would be placed on the floor, it was polished hardwood with no rugs or carpets.

After the second chair, he saw a small triangle of blood, probably made by the toe of a shoe. He had not seen any mark in the blood around the woman, no it wouldn't be that easy. This small mark was not enough to trace to someone's shoe. It did confirm his hunch that the killer left in the rear direction.

Following the fading trail of marks, he was soon heading down a hallway that led to the kitchen. Pushing through the swinging doors, he was in a large modern cooking area with half-made platters deserted on counters. Everyone had fled at the first warning of shots or panic. They left through the back doors, and no cops had been in that area to stop or question anyone.

By the time Bower made his way to the back door and through it, there were a couple of black and whites with lights blazing and cops walking around, but no kitchen help in sight.

Feeling like he was in one of those high school tests that he always failed, he didn't even take time to talk to the blues, he just shook his head and returned inside. Joining Rob all the way back to the first body, the people all in white were doing their job. Cameras flashed, cases were open, and lines were being drawn.

"Sir, you need to step outside." A person that was probably a Chief in the probing CSI group peeked out of his white hoodie at Bower.

Showing his gold shield on his belt, Bower did stay back out of the way. "I only need a guess of the size of the weapon that killed our vics?"

"Well," said a man kneeling but unidentifiable due to the all-white suit. I haven't taken a good look at the other two, but my guess and it's only a guess, I would say from my experience, it was a forty-five."

"Hey." It was the Chief, about to throw his weight around. "There is no way we can confirm anything yet. Ignore what that man said."

Holding up his hands, Bower began to back away. "Easy, I was only asking. By the way, how long has he been on the job?" One of Bower's long fingers pointed at the man kneeling who had made the intelligent guess.

"You don't have to worry. We are all well-trained professionals." The Chief proffered with a huff. "He has been on the job for over ten years."

"Great, and when did you get your deserved promotion?" Bower asked from the door as he was leaving.

"I was promoted three months ago."

Before there was any more conversation, Bower was gone and back in the big room. Charlie was standing like a statue, waiting for orders, with tears on his cheeks. This was one of the things that had turned him away from these games. Bower understood that all the players had feelings and that what happened to their mental make-up was going downhill in these games.

Although Bower had never been to this particular club, they all had the same layout. He shook his head as he ran through the numbers that were not in the paycheck of a detective. Ten thousand memberships to get through that front door unless you had a special invitation. At two clubs, Bower had invitations that he no longer used.

CHAPTER TWO

Because of Bower's experience, he had been assigned to an undercover sting on one club where the division of slave trafficking needed additional personnel. But the rooms were all the same. In that first room, all cell phones, cameras, and recording devices were taken and held securely for the clients. Bower knew better than to check the house for any visual records of the crime, as secrecy was part of the game.

Using the word *game* gave a chill to his back as he remembered his first introduction into BDSM and how he thought it would be his last. It wasn't. It was like his choice of being a cop. He kept saying no and went on to be the best he could, which was often better than most. There was this silly voice inside that would not accept failure or even second best.

As he ran this through his mind, he realized Charlie was following him, two paces behind and on the left. It was the standard sub-position.

"Charley, did you know the three people who were killed?" Bower used the Master tone, deciding he might as well play the role and get good info.

"Yes, M, uh, Detective," Charlie answered with his head lowered. "The man in the lobby is Dr. Frank Stellar. The lady there"—he gulped—"is or was Mistress Martha Saluda and the gentleman on the cross is Donald Prentice."

Yes, Bower thought, the paid submissive servers would know everyone. Yet, as they worked and did their jobs, they were almost invisible. He shook his head, knowing Charlie would not understand the gesture. That was one of the things that had turned him away from this lifestyle. There was that period of the game when everyone was different for a time and could pretend to be someone else.

For his life, he preferred the real thing and to finish a puzzle, not to create it. Here, he had an interesting puzzle. A member or a person with an invitation came through the lobby. At this point, Bower looked past Charlie and the large opening to the room. The walls were covered with real red velvet material. When the bright lights were off, the walls would look dark or black and absorb noise to keep the large room quiet and cozy.

Due to the thick walls and doors and sound suppressions used on the walls and ceilings in this club, it was likely that no one heard the loud shot of the forty-five out front. The killer came into this large, crowded room, which was dim with red lights behind the bar and artificial candles on each table.

There had been low beam spotlights on the exhibition sights. But the killer was used to the room because he had been able to approach his intended victim with the gun out before anyone noticed except the girl. Bower decided the true casualty was the man on the cross, Donald Prentice. The girl was collateral damage or perhaps was a weak bodyguard. Puzzles and puzzles, Bower was in his happy place, except he felt terrible about the dead people.

Well, to appease his conscience, he promised the three of them to do his best to track down their shooter. He again appraised the trail of chairs the suspect left as they ran. The heavy armless furniture all had thick caps of smooth rubber on each leg to keep them quiet on the hard, shiny wood floor.

The automatic fake candles still flickered in their round glass containers, some slid out of place from the center of each table. There were these same fake candles on wall hooks and along the bar. There was a smell of honey and sex that was over the odor of blood as the automatic air conditioning in the club was still working.

"Okay, Charlie, I know others have asked you, but look at me." Bower waited for the thin male to raise his eyes. "I am the one asking now." Bower was using his Dom full-on as he looked down but with no expression, only his blue eyes meeting Charlie's. "Did you see the person with the gun who did the shooting?"

"No, Master."

Waiting a couple of seconds, Bower kept their gazes locked. "Did you see someone running toward the back?"

Now Charlie looked down, but he cleared his throat and finally got the nerve to answer. "It wasn't a member. It was a man, tall but not as tall as you, with black hair."

"You did good, Charlie. You can kiss my foot." Bower stood stiff, and the grateful, smiling male dropped down to slobber over one shoe. At that moment, Bower looked up to see the Forensics Chief and Rob coming into the room.

Knowing there was no need to say anything to the sub, and he was sure as hell that he was not going to try to explain himself to the snobbish chief, he moved around Charlie and waited.

Behind him, Charlie got up and quietly left the room through the troubling back exit.

Taking a big sigh, Rob moved over to her tall partner, not going to ask anything.

But the Chief was mumbling about fool detectives as several more white-covered people came in and spread out. They started by ignoring the two bodies, looking for all the trace evidence around the death scene. One guy was taking pictures with a flash that blinked fast, so it must have been a digital camera, even though it was large.

This team was good as they carefully covered all the outside detail, had glasses left half full on the bar, and spilled ashtrays on the floor near the wall.

After an hour with Bower standing still and out of the way, at last they had placed a lot of makers, so they began the collection process.

As people now worked on the bodies, Rob moved over to her partner, holding up her tablet. "Let's hope they get fingerprints first. No one claims to know the deceased."

"The guy in front is Dr. Frank Stellar." Rob hesitated and then typed the name into the pad as Bower continued. "The girl is Martha Saluda, and the man on the cross is Donald Prentice."

"Okay, partner." Rob kept her voice low so the forensic team wouldn't hear. "No one would talk. How did you get the works?"

Smiling, Bower looked down at her boots. "You should have let them kiss the toes of your boots."

Now, they both looked down and chuckled. As detectives in Precinct Thirty-Three, which was on the rough side of the city, they were allowed to dress in civilian clothes, which meant they could blend into the neighborhoods.

With his long black leather coat, Bower wore stressed denims, and ankle high zippered boots. He usually wore a dark tee shirt or sweater, depending on the weather.

As for his partner, she had on dark cargo pants that were sold in Second-Hand stores and high lace boots with the pants tucked in. She got them from the SWAT team.

But now, Bower's interest was on the body of Martha Saluda. At last, the forensic team was carefully turning her over to check for evidence under the body. He also was interested to know where her little gun had come from and if it had been fired.

The pistol was carefully taken from the hand and a special bag was placed over to enclose all the way above the wrist.

One snap and the bag pulled tight at the top to seal in place. The gun was also secured in an evidence bag that was clear with a red seal at the top. The man made some quick notes on the top of the gun bag and took it over to a collection box.

Puzzles, puzzles, puzzles. The few outside friends that Bower had assumed that he had got into police work to fight and wrestle the bad guys. But his real reason was the way his mind worked. When he discovered that detective work was seventy percent paper trails and following puzzles, he found his home.

Unfortunately, he would have to wait for most of the forensic reports to come together to hit his desk computer. He had a lot of pertinent information already that no one else had picked up on. He knew there was only one killer, and it was the male who had left through the back door.

All these private clubs might not allow any cameras, but they all kept excellent records on income and that related to paying members and any complimentary visitors. A special visitor's pass had to be issued in place of the membership's gold card.

There was a plan cooking in Bower's mind that his boss would not approve, so he decided not to share it with his partner. "I think I'll head back to the precinct and wait for the reports to start coming in to the computers. It will be at least twelve hours before we have anything from the morgue."

He had a friend down in the autopsy department that might get him snips of information before that time, but he kept that tidbit private.

"You got your tablet in your car?" Rob asked without looking up.

"As always. Notify me of any important items." Bower decided to go out the back door.

"As always."

He heard his partner with a smile while he made his way

to the back of this cub through an area that the members with lots of money and strange ideas never saw. He wanted to think like the killer, but instead, he got chills and felt his stomach want to leave another trail.

By the time he pushed the back door open and let the fresh night air settle his body, he had to pull his coat aside. Two cops were about to draw on him by the time he had his badge on his belt in sight. It took him a couple of seconds to slow his heart. One of the first things he had learned was to keep an impassive emotion on his face. People expected a handsome, tall man never to be frightened or angry.

It had taken him three years of fight training, during which, in the first two years, he got his ass kicked royally before he learned to fight back. It was his final teacher that told him, that it was his mind holding him back and to release the anger Bower was afraid of and held. He still hated to fight, but when he did, he expected to win.

Now he wanted to win this battle to find this killer, as he walked around the only direction to leave the back of the club. There was a surprise.

CHAPTER THREE

From the corner to the front of the club, a line of taxis, limos, and high-priced cars, their drivers being held by various street cops, followed by a long line of black and whites with red and blue lights blazing, along with the wagons for Forensics and now the media. Everything is blocked in at this time.

But when that first loud forty-five went off, how many left? How many escaped to waiting cars down the street or taxis that didn't ask questions? Bower had one answer — the killer. Either he had planned it all out well or had been lucky. Bower bet on a well-planned assassination.

Keeping his coat back so everyone could see the gold shield, he crossed the street and walked down an alley. He and Rob were old hands to a public death scene, and they both parked one street away. This prevented them from getting trapped in all of the investigative vehicles. Now, it was easy to find his personal ride.

Walking between the six and eight-story buildings in the dark alley, Bower was familiar with this type of neighborhood. At one time, the buildings were full, and the top floors were rented to families or working singles. The middle levels were full of company or professional offices, and the first floors were open with stores and delis.

Now, this dark alley with trash moving in the wind was a testament to the buildings on both sides. Most windows had no lights showing, and some were broken, especially up high. The stores were empty and closed with boarded-up fronts, and many had street people sleeping inside. Once a board had been pried enough to allow a tired, cold body to get in, the rest followed.

This represented the area Bower and the Precinct Thirty-Three were in charge of. The sex club and several other bars were located across the street. It was a divided line of the edge of the surviving city and the rest of this area with the loss of jobs.

That street, which was the line between those who had and those who despaired, was what Bower saw as his life. So, he worked homicide, which was mostly a night shift, and he solved puzzles. Somewhere in there, he hoped he accomplished some good.

As he came out onto the littered sidewalk, with small bits of paper tossed by the wind and, on this street, most of the lights busted, he shook his head. Three mangy, dressed-out teen gang hangers were leaning against his car.

His car drew the attention of anyone under forty, but especially the young ones yearned for this Ford Police Interceptor Mustang that had no frills but all the looks of speed. The one thing these young toughs had already found out was that the car could not be unlocked by inserting that thin hook between the glass and the door to find the catch. This one had an actual electronic lock.

Not changing his walk, he moved right up to the car and shoved one kid out of the way.

"What the hell." Bower made his voice a growl. "Which one of you idiots scratched my window?" Now he slowly took the leather coat off, and the thugs could see the Magnum pistol that was larger than the Glock that was a police issue. As he turned, they could also see the gold shield.

Someone muttered, "A fucken cop," and the group began to move away. Once they had some room, they began to run, and it was to see who was the fastest or who might get caught by the tall man who owned the GUCCI car.

In peace, Bower used his thumbprint to unlock the car. He threw his coat in the back and slid into the seat that hugged him. The seats were made of strong, fire-resistant material that conformed to the body. This entire vehicle was produced to protect and help police and was particularly used by the Highway Patrol across the country, which had long chases at very high speeds.

But Bower had found it useful at tight corners and speeding between traffic. It was the only one owned by the City Police Department and considered too expensive and not city worthy for considering purchase. This one had been stolen out of Detroit and had very few miles on it when Bower's department had tracked a killer down to where the vehicle trailer was being stored.

The killer belonged to a gang that was auctioning off the Mustang. But they went online with the auction, and the Police Cyber department tipped off everyone. Bower led the raid with the biggest warrant on the killer.

Taking one look at that dull black car, he knew it was his. Evidently, Detroit left the special high-powered, special-wheel vehicle that color so that whatever Police Department bought it would find it easy to paint in their official colors. But on the night shift, it was the perfect color when Bower first saw it. A few hidden blue and red lights done by friends in the back garage, and he loved his ride. So did the young thugs.

Once he was comfortable with a cold bottle of water, he popped up the standard built-in police computer. It sat between the driver and passenger seats near the dashboard on a swivel that could be turned or tilted.

Once he turned it on, he remembered why he hated the thing. There were all kinds of notices, some he could ignore and some he needed. The one from Dispatch could wait, the two from Rob were important even though they had only been apart for a short while. But the one from the boss was a pain in the ass that he had to answer immediately.

Holding his finger over the one button that would put him right back through to the boss, he still waited. Naw, it could wait to see what Rob had to drop in his box. Rob might have info he could give to the boss. What a coward he was, he shook his head as he opened his Dropbox.

There were two files from Rob and the first was only that the Morgue Vehicle had arrived. The second stated that the young woman had fired one shot, but they found it lodged in a wall. There were no other bullets found lodged anywhere.

Nodding to himself, he felt he was beginning to hate this killer. Not only did he make a clean get away, but he was an accurate shot.

Not being able to think of any other excuse, he hit the sticky button, and as usual, he was put right through.

"Ah, Detective Reed Bower, so nice to hear from you." The man's voice didn't sound nice.

"Been a little busy out on the streets, boss." Bower kept his voice low, hoping to keep the conversation with Captain Martin short.

"The DA reamed my ass because the evidence on the Belcher trial reached them late." There was a long sigh from the Captain's end.

"Things happen, boss." Bower didn't think that it would help to take the time to tell everything they had gone through to trace down the last guy and rush the disk over to the courthouse.

*

First of all, Bower and Rob had been told to pick up a person who was supposed to testify and transport him. They had plenty of time until they reached the address and three guys with automatics. They had a different idea.

They were there to eliminate the informant but were only street thugs and hired quickly. One of them fired as soon as Rob knocked on the door, but the bullets missed her as her training let her stand at the side. Still, both of them were surprised at the rain of holes in the wood and the flakes that appeared on the opposite wall.

Looking at his partner, he'd winked. "Okay, most of the SWAT team is in the back. We will bust the door and send in a grenade and kill everyone. On Three." Bower was shouting loud, but also through the mic that repeated through Rob's shoulder speaker.

"One." Bower's voice echoed down the hall as the door was pulled open. A guy who needed a bath threw his automatic across the floor and out into the hallway.

"You won't hurt me because there are rules for policemen." The guy looked over his shoulder down the hall.

With the head turned, Bower slugged him unconscious with his big gun. "Yeah, that's what my Captain keeps telling me."

It took them another few minutes to wrap up the other two men who had surrendered, pleading that no one would throw a grenade. Now there was a wait for a couple of black and whites to pick up the three idiots. Of course, they were late delivering the informant, but they still got him there alive. They also called an ambulance for the security cop who was watching the informant and was unconscious in a closet.

"You know, Detective Bower," Captain Martin wasn't through. "I would fire your ass right now if you weren't the best person on the job. Tell me about Club La Masque."

"We got the identity of the three that were killed and the size of the weapon. I think it was one person. We need to get copies of all street cameras and any possible back alley ones within the two-block area. The killer left through the rear."

Now, he waited for the Captain to react.

"As usual, you are ahead of Forensics. Okay, I will get on all warrants for copies of any private views. You can pull up the street cameras through the police files, and Detective Bower check in more often." The Captain cut the call.

Taking the time to read the notices from Dispatch, he didn't find anything important. Most of it was notices about all local officers to report to shooting at 4044 Madison Ave. That was the address for the sex club La Masque.

There was one urging Bower to return to Headquarters, but everyone knew he seldom used the cubby that he and Rob shared. Now came the work that he loved and no one else understood from watching the TV shows. Solving the puzzle.

That meant hours of digging deep into the lives of the three people that were deceased and looking to tie them to a killer. It would take him hours and hours to chase through the records he had to pull with legal help from the club.

There would be a personal view of the autopsies and reading in depth the reports from the good hands on the Pathologist who handled Dr. Frank Stellar.

The one thing Bower knew from his own instincts was that if he took the time and put all of that together, somewhere buried in all of those reports, audits, reviews, and talking to any and all people, a solid clue would appear.

Ever since, as a teen, when he out grew all the guys, and his good looks attracted too many females, people judged him wrong. Every woman thought he was made for loving, but most of the guys saw a chance to brag about beating the fuck out of the big guy. No one noticed his high scores in school and scholarships to college.

They never commented on the fact that he dated a few ladies and got in a few fights. He did take rare training in oriental fighting and found Tai Chi to calm him and let him control his long legs and arms. It was by accident, when he changed to criminal studies in college, that he met a young man who introduced him to one of the rare studios run by a Chinese immigrant.

When Bower could, he avoided a fight, but when he did fight, he was deadly. His big body moved in fast, smooth moves that were unexpected and hit his opponent to disable or stop the ruckus. It worked.

Now, Bower used that training to relax his body and settle his mind so he could do what he wanted—find the beginning of the puzzle. He began to build his layout on his computer, starting at the top with the large bold question mark. ? That would be the last that would be changed when he reached his quest and settled his hatred of such people, killers, or, this time, one killer.

CHAPTER FOUR

Now, he had the names of the three killed, the club, and the items he needed to examine in detail. Each of these titles would eventually have lots of simple notes added. He had a special phone that he programmed into this computer with one button.

Starting up the car that purred, he drove a couple of blocks to the better part of town and went through a drive through that was open twenty-four hours every day. Moving into a quiet spot in the parking lot of a closed dress store, he settled down to eat and see if Police Central had pulled up any cameras.

The street cameras for the hours before and after the police call came up immediately. These were constantly rolling and the tapes were on files for some time.

Rob, doing her job too efficiently, had forwarded him the copies of the driver's license she had pulled with her heavy-duty tablet from Police Central. There was a cross street light that caught a photo every twenty seconds. It had a wide view to catch street racers, which had been a problem in the area. It also showed the well-lit street on the north side and the many boarded places on the south side of the wide pavement.

Watching the cars passing through was like blinking too much in a movie, but it did pay off. In the short camera shots, Bower could see some cars turn into the club's side parking lot and disappear. But there were others that stopped at the front, and someone or more would get out. In jerking motions, a porter would move the car as the patrons entered.

Due to the distance, the lights, and the quick short blinks, it was hard to identify the clients, but a nice Porsche pulled up, and a lady in a dark suit entered the club. Freezing one of the shots and blowing it up, Bower knew he was looking at Martha Saluda.

Going backward to older street cameras, he got the plate number on the expensive car and added it under her name on his computer. He also added the time she had entered the club. Watching for hours, he never caught a view of the two men, Stellar and Prentice, entering the club through the front door.

The sky was changing color, so he sent a note to Rob, telling her about finding Saluda's entrance. He also added that he was knocking off for the night. With that, there was a load of items from her in his Dropbox, but he would check everything out with his breakfast. His mind was getting foggy, and he needed some real sleep.

What Bower called home was near Precinct Thirty-Three. That meant it was what those who had regular jobs and a good place to sleep would call the wrong side of town. The rent was cheap since everyone was moving out or not paying, and the guy that owned the place was grateful to have a cop on the premises.

It was a two-room plus bath above the garage where he kept the car. For him, it was perfect, as a person had to go through the garage and three awkward doors to get to the narrow stairs. There was no more, just a door at the top that opened out.

The garage was empty, with no boxes or tool chests. A couple of hooks held some coats, and that was all he stored beside a hose and a broom. The apartment was almost as bare. A super large mattress on the floor with too many covers and pillows made it hard to decide which was front or back.

The so-called kitchen area was empty except for a lot of

disposable cups and a fancy automatic coffee maker. One of those types that let him make good coffee fast, either one cup or more. Coffee was essential to Bower, it kept him from drinking.

He carried several devils on his wide shoulders, and one was alcohol. There was a time when he hid both his glee and his anger in a bottle. Now, he knew his weakness and felt he could not stop with one.

Kicking off his boots after making it up to his room, he could still smell the odor of the exhaust of his car below. He tried to remember to shut the car off as soon as possible since there was very little between the apartment floor and the garage.

Smelling his sweat as he headed toward the shower, between that and the memory of the guy on the cross at the club, brought back when he had used such a room to put on a show. It was in a different club, and the owner, Mistress Romana, had backed him into a corner with a challenge.

A friend had invited him, a man who was a paid client, and Bower was officially invited. Bower had tasted this life because a woman he thought he cared about pleaded for him to become her Dom. It took him a bit to check it out through books and movies, but the second time in real life with her was nothing. He lost his respect for her, and she found someone else who liked tying her up.

But to help a friend out who was hunting for his sister, he put on his motorcycle boots with the chains, tight leather pants that he pushed low on his hips, and tore the sleeves off a black tee shirt. Unfortunately, his looks brought the owner out of her office and over to their table for too much attention.

While Mistress Romana flirted and edged Bower to do a public demonstration, his friend quietly encouraged him. This gave his friend a chance to look closely at each sub that was brought into the room, trying to find his sis.

The sub the Mistress brought forward was beautiful and completely into the game. She was almost naked and tanned in places most women never exposed to the sun. The idea was that he tied her on the cross and, by using a whip or talking, but not touching her private parts, brought her to an orgasm.

Remembering that beautiful woman who accepted the fact that she was naked and displayed under a bright light in front of forty or fifty people. Bower never told his friend it wasn't his words that brought her to her peak. It was what they all thought as he whispered to her, as he touched her softly with the leather on the whip and only said her name in each ear when he moved around her. It was her excitement that caused her to jerk and her hips to move forward. Everyone saw the look of release on her face as he walked away.

As a cop, he would say if it wasn't against a written law and involved consenting adults, leave it alone. But he found he no longer was interested in that particular lady and her way of life and sex. He preferred something simpler and between only two of them, and there was no need for extras except for a condom.

Returning to the BDSM life only again had been as an investigator when the unit required volunteers who had experience. Bower was the only one capable of getting an invitation to the club on the river that was a cover for slave trade.

Fortunately, a good sleep in the room with the heavy mismatched drapes over the high windows, left him ready to work on his puzzle. Doing all the routine things to get ready for work, he went down to the car, hit the button to open the garage door, and reported through the car's computer that he was on duty.

There was a notice of dozens of new items in his Dropbox, plus the usual flags from Central, the Captain, and people in general. Ignoring everything until he had his coffee, he drove to the best drive thru for the large black double shot and a blueberry muffin.

As usual, since it was nighttime, he found a parking spot next door at a small strip mall with everything closed. Now, he could open the computer with his large tablet. His first choice was to pull up Rob's emails and notes, as she was great at her job.

From her first note, he went to the top of his puzzle and filled in the complete identities of the three deceased. Dr. Frank Stellar was a retired physician from a large local hospital, and his address put him out in the suburbs. Bower marked him as collateral damage, but he still had a big question mark. What had this older man done to get one clean hole in his forehead?

Mrs. Saluda was a divorced lady who was an attorney with a very prominent firm. Her address put her in one of the exclusive tall apartment buildings near the park. She was worth a lot of money as she came from one of the investment families that had moved in about thirty years ago. Her records stated she also earned a big salary with the law firm.

The question mark still by her, Bower had to wonder why such a successful and beautiful lady carried a gun. Rob's digging had discovered a carry permit for the small twenty-two.

The last information pulled from records was in a different direction. It was on Donald Prentice, and first, there was an inquiry from out of state from a worried wife. The records showed that Prentice was a successful real estate investor from Tampa, Florida.

Now, there was where a lot of question marks were up. Who and why would want a Florida realtor dead?

Well, that was all the fun. Bower got out of the car and returned to the busy restaurant. This time, he went inside, dumped his trash in a barrel, used the restroom, and left with another strong coffee.

Now, he was sitting comfortably in the car and looking at camera views. They had been able to get copies of two alley cameras and Rob sent him a notice of street cameras that covered the alley's exit.

It was over four hours and a trip through a new fast food shop with a trip to the restroom before he saw a man running in the dark street. Unfortunately, no matter how he worked the computer and the view, the face could not be seen.

Working until his supper time or third meal, Bower played with the view, stopping it and locking it into one instant at a time. He did get a lot of information. The man wore running shoes that measured size men's eleven.

Using the known height of a street light and a stop sign, he could soon find out that the man was five foot eleven or six foot tall. Due to the way the man ran, he was athletic and strong. And where was the gun? The man was running in a light jacket and slacks that were dark in color. That forty-five had to be large and heavy. It would bounce, or the outline would show. Nope, no gun, but Bower believed this was his killer.

Now, he needed to return with several street cops to the back entrance of the club. The tedious search for the weapon had to be done, but this time on the outside. Bower had confidence in Rob and the team she assembled to search inside, especially after he shared with her his decision the killer left through the rear.

There were six cops and Bower to search all along the alley out to the main street. They were waiting for him to lay out the instructions, and he was looking at six sets of bored eyes. There were three large dumpsters, one next to the rear door of the club and the other two scattered down in the dark near other doors. There were three sets of white coveralls, plus booties and heavy rubber gloves for the ones who searched those stinking monsters.

Seeing the negative frowns on these cops, Bower had to do something to get them on the job. He went back to the kitchen and opened the cold rooms. In the second one, he found what he wanted—a fully sealed case of bottled beer. Going back out, he stood up on the case, looked over the group, and began his pep talk.

"As you have already been told, the people inside were killed with a forty-five. These are not small weapons, and we found a camera view that we believe is a shot of the possible perp, but he didn't have the weapon on him. The camera was a standard street police camera and no close up." Now, he stopped and looked down the back alley with the trash bins and doors and windows.

"This guy is intelligent and planned out his hit. He went through the club within minutes, from the front door to this exit, which tells us that he did a recon before as he made his plan. That means he also planned to dump the weapon somewhere so it would not be on him if he were stopped.

"This guy thinks he is smarter than us, so we need to think outside the box that he thinks he has us in. Getting into the trash bins is ugly, but I will take the first one to prove that a detective can get down and dirty to solve a crime."

That brought a couple of chuckles and some nods. It was the right thing to say. He stepped down and then stopped.

"Oh, by the way. The person that finds the weapon wins this case of cold beer on me." Bower tapped the case with a boot and then turned to start getting dressed in white.

He could hear some side bets going on as two more men came over to join him in the protective covers. In some way, they had lost an original bet and would have to search the garbage. Still, one of them had been lucky as a bin was outside a dress shop full of boxes, rags, and leftovers. It was full and needed searching but it wasn't stinking.

Bower and the third one were outside kitchens, accumulating smells from previous loads. The first layer of bags wasn't bad, but going down was digging into hell. Figuring he had been digging for an hour and a half or more and breathing through his mouth to avoid the smell when there was a loud tap on the outside.

Glad of the excuse to ease his back, he was careful to have his feet on something solid and stood. With the few inches the rollers under the bin added and whatever he was standing on, Bower looked down at one of the cops. Most of them had taken off their heavy jackets and caps but still wore their belts with their Glocks.

"Detective, we have an officer who says he would like a beer." This was a cop who had been around for a while and probably liked serving in blue. He had a half smile on his face that did look serious.

CHAPTER FIVE

Taking the cop at his word and attitude, Bower climbed out of the large bin and kept his gloves on until he had the overalls and booties off and over with the rest of the smelling stuff. At last, he pulled off the gloves and added them inside as he followed the guy with good news.

About twenty feet from the back exit of the club, they now joined the other five who were standing around a large box up against the back wall.

"Okay." Bower frowned at the group. "Where's the weapon?"

Like a chorus line, they turned as one, and all raised their left hand, almost like a salute, to point upward. He looked up, and there was a wide trim board about ten feet above. Probably at one time, it hid the rain pipes, but modern installation with new ones up above left the board as trim only.

"So, he pushed a box over there. Funny, I didn't see that when we started." Now, Bower used his height to add a bit of pressure as he questioned the cops.

"Nope." One guy reached down and pulled the box out of the way. Another turned his flash on, highlighting what looked like a scuff mark on the wall. It was about where a healthy man would leave a mark if he were jumping up and using the wall to help give him an actual boost. In his mind, Bower saw the man in the grey camera view use those strong legs for a quick jump.

"My kids leave the same mark as they climb back into their room after hours." The guy who explained the mark pushed the tall wooden crate over. "Want to see. We didn't touch anything."

Climbing up on the crate took an extra push after his muscles were still from the bending down in the trash barrel. But his extra height did give him a nice view of the barrel of a forty-five as he held his flashlight up above the ledge.

With one jump, he was down. "Good job. Someone go and get Forensics. We need pictures and fingerprints. Also." He turned to the cop with a family. "The beer is yours."

As he started down the alley, he sent off a note to Rob to bring her up on the find of the forty-five. Behind him, he overheard a statement.

"Okay, one beer apiece, but the rest goes home with me." Six cops got to relax after doing a good job. It should always have ended like that, but it didn't.

He suggested to Rob via iPhone that they return to Precinct Thirty-Three and appease the Captain by clocking in and spending a couple hours at their desks.

By the time he pulled into one of the reserved spots at the back of the building, where he did not have a tag to use, he saw Rob's big van.

Glancing across the wide pavement between the front building and the huge garage, with the doors all up and lights blazing, a night crew was working on vehicles. Rob was probably getting gas and a cleaning on the inside. She carried a lot of interesting things in that van and was fussy about keeping everything pristine and in order.

As for his special Interceptor, it was a hog for fuel, so he filled it each time he was near the garage. He would swing by the gas pumps on his way out after working with Rob upstairs.

Going up to what was listed as the second floor, which was three stories above due to the high ceiling on the first, in the back was a large area for detectives and special divisions. Even though the different groups were divided, they often shared and borrowed people.

If you didn't know, it would be hard to tell the police from those who were arrested and on hold in this section of the building. First of all, the dress code was non-existent. In fact, only two men and a woman were dressed in business clothes, with their jackets off and their badges and official Glocks in belt holsters. From there, it was like watching a movie of the Street People.

Bower smiled and felt right at home as he slipped out of his leather coat and let the big Magnum be revealed. His boots and jeans were seen on a lot of men and women up here. There was also long hair and beards on men and wild hair color on some women. This area was where the detectives often had to blend in to catch the real top of the chain.

This was the area where Special Ops had a leader in one of the side offices and many teammates in dark, torn clothes working at desks outside that space. Drugs and Illegal Meds was off in a corner, and there was a mix of people, from some who looked like teens to some who were clean and might be someone's neighbor.

There was the High Crime Division, and that was where the better-dressed people were. There were a lot more computers and equipment, and some crowded into the Captain's larger office.

In this massive room with so many intelligent people, there was even room for two groups that were working next to each other. It was the Slaves and Child misuse and Computer Tracing or hackers. There was so much done with electronics these days that these two groups now took up more room than any of the others. But most of the time, most of them never went out into the field. They provided the information and proof for the other departments to chase with rights perps.

That area got more contact and traffic from all the other detectives because of their ability to trace anyone or anything. Bower did make a stop past that section that had a whole lot of open letter drops. Sure enough, in the one with his name, among many others, were some print outs.

It took him almost fifteen minutes to walk across the expansive room, with many square structure support posts every so often that never separated the desks or divisions correctly.

Rob was sitting with her feet propped up on her desk, working on the heavy-duty pad she preferred to a computer. There was no chest-high divider between them, as folders and items slid easily back and forth as they worked together.

Before he even relaxed back in his chair, Rob threw a picture over onto the large flat screen on his desk. It was the forty-five.

"You sure know how to pick a team of boys in blue. Under two hours, and they found the killer's weapon."

He smiled at his partner's snide comment. "I think it was the case of cold beer that found the hiding place." Moving closer, he began to read the reports. "Yep," Bower sat back and sighed. "He was too smart to leave any fingerprints."

"Yes, but . . ." Rob had another picture on his desk screen. It was only a strange blob. "He left the print of his shoe. An expensive buy at a sports store. Now the smart boys in the computer lab are tracing the wear on that toe."

"Hey. It's not much, but we have sent them up on less. Let's go over all the reports again. Did they get a warrant for the private cameras in the area?" Bower set up his larger phone, which he made notes on, so he could transfer everything over to his puzzle page.

Now, the two well-paid and smart detectives would sit for hours and do what no one ever saw on TV or in the movies.

They looked at camera views, one shot at a time. Report after report was put into different piles and folders. Some were important and would be gone over again. Others didn't seem to have any relation to the incident but would be kept. These extras still had to be examined and logged into notes in case something came up later to tie them in with a small bit.

After an hour, Rob went to the restroom, and Bower went to fill his cup full of coffee from the offering on a long cabinet. There were several automatics that made a large cup at a time and always several people with their cups in place, but there were enough machines, so the wait was short. On the end of the counter was a box of donuts and Bower's favorite slices of banana nut bread.

Going through two more coffees and getting past supper time on the night shift, Bower turned to his partner.

"Hey, partner. Let's leave and talk to real people. We need some food, and then it will be late enough to swing by the sex club. I bet the owner or manager is over there, working whatever papers Forensics left behind."

Gathering up folders and her special large tablet, Rob was getting ready to go, which meant she agreed. "We need to get up early tomorrow evening and talk to some of the people related to the deceased, also."

They went into an all-night restaurant, and while they ate, they both made suggestions of who to talk to first. They took their own cars as they swung by the club, which still had several black-and-whites in front and yellow tape over the sidewalk.

"Anyone inside besides the police?" Bower approached one of the guys in blue as he ducked under the yellow tape.

"The owner is in her office. The Captain sent word it was okay. She went in through a private door at the parking lot side." The cop pointed over to the side of the building that Bower and Rob had not looked into. As they walked around the corner of the building, they saw a large parking lot between the club and its neighbor. There were a couple of lights high up on the club side and only two cars in the lot. One was next to a plain door with signs that said, NO ENTRANCE, EXIT ONLY. The other was several spots closer to the street and probably belonged to a client that hadn't claimed it yet. They had reports on the three vehicles of the deceased that had been towed to the Precinct garage.

The parking area had not been taped off, so the car near the door with the signs probably belonged to the person they needed to get some questions and answers from now.

Bower tried the door, and when it opened, he stepped back to hold it for his partner to enter. He did see her automatically place her hand on her weapon, but she didn't draw.

What they were entering was a short hall with a fluorescent light that was almost too bright for the small area. It opened into a T hall that was also short with doors on each end. One had the look of hinges and probably went into storage, they turned to the other and without knocking, opened it to find an office.

Unlike the opulence of the club, this was a working place. The large desk filled most of the area with many matching metal file cabinets along two walls. There was a short cabinet with files and what looked like glasses on top. Next to it was another door.

There was only one guest chair in front of the desk, and a lady was looking up from behind it with a frown. "The police were supposed to keep everyone away." Her tone was almost an order.

Rob bristled, but Bower recognized the tone of a Dom. Using the same tone and standing with his feet apart and his hands on his hips, he answered.

"I'm Detective Bower, and this is Detective Pervis." The stance pushed his coat back to reveal the gold shield on his belt. Rob pulled out her police wallet and flipped it open to reveal hers. Then putting it away, she flipped open the metal cover of her large tablet. "Are you Joella Margret Reviv?"

"Of course, who else would be sitting at this desk?"

Bower had to shrug, this was going to be fun, and this woman was going to be in real pain. "Look, lady." Bower stepped forward and leaned down on the desk to put his face directly into the boss's. "We have a killer to find and maybe keep him away from you. Now, what we want to know, and we want it fast. Who was the Dom that put Prentice on the Cross? We also need the sub of Saluda and the sub or Dom of Dr. Stellar."

First, the woman started to react as a Dom against a Dom in her territory. It looked like she was going to rise out of the chair and make this a pissing contest.

"No," Bower said, the word low but almost a hiss. "This might be your place, but we have the power. We can keep you closed down for as long as we want for any excuse, including withholding information. It would be better if the word went out that the Club La Masque was fully cooperating to protect its patrons and help find the person who did this terrible deed on their property."

At last, Bower raised one eyebrow and straightened back up. He waited a moment to give the woman who ran a world of kink and pain to decide the right direction. But even if Joella was deep into strange stuff, she was still a very intelligent person. He heard the deep sigh and knew they were going to get what they need.

There were the lines where the computer had been taken by Forensics, but this lady had backups.

"I need to get something from my bag." The lady pointed to a large handbag that was sitting on the low chest.

"Wait," Rob reacted. She went over and got the bag, and opened it, probably checking for a weapon. What she did pull out of was a small tablet that reminded Bower of the type people read a lot of novels on or watched movies late at night.

"Is this what you're looking for?" Rob handed the small pad to Joella.

Not bothering to reply, the woman took the pad and booted it up. Looking up at Bower as an equal, she raised both eyebrows. "I had a lot of stuff backed up on hidden places in the cloud. Now, let's see." She began to scroll and then tap one letter at a time on the keyboard that appeared at the bottom of the small screen.

CHAPTER SIX

Without a lot of conversation, the two detectives left with three names and addresses. They now had a list of places to visit when they started their shift early tomorrow.

Pulling up behind Rob's van in front of the high-end duplex, Bower was on his second cup of high-kick coffee and still hated being awake at six in the evening. Although he had promised himself to turn in early, he had spent too much time filling in his notes and completing the puzzle of the Masque murders on his tablet. Looking at his self-made puzzle was a mistake. He got caught up in filling notes up and down and ended up with only five hours of sleep.

The first stop was the residence of Dr. Frank Stellar, who, unfortunately, had probably been collateral damage of the attack at the sex club. Why he had been killed had still not been answered. Had he recognized the killer or perhaps seen a man with a weapon? Puzzles within puzzles.

But the doctor was well off since this was a residence on the better side of town and was worth a lot. Going together up the steps to the fancy, wide double doors, both of them had their shields on display. A maid answered the door and had a large black band on her arm. She led them through the clean, high-ceiling rooms to a side parlor where there were two women hugging and crying.

As the two separated, both Bower and Rob stopped and looked at each other, hesitating to speak.

Separating, the older but still very attractive woman

straightened up and spoke, and she rose from the sofa. "Oh, the police. Yes, I was told you would need to talk to me." Like a gracious hostess, but with wet cheeks and red eyes, she waved a hand at some love seats at one side. "Please sit, and I will answer what I can. Oh, this is the daughter of a friend, and she has stayed with me. She feels the same loss I do."

Letting his gaze travel over the younger woman, Bower bit his lip. The younger woman matched the description and Driver's License photo of Dr. Stellar's sub at the sex club. They had pulled photos of all the people they were going to interview and did a deeper address check on everyone.

To say it was a surprise to find a sex submissive at the home and with the wife of a Dom was not something that happened. But it looked like something unusual was going on at this Doctor's residence.

"Mrs. Stellar." Bower took a seat and motioned to Rob, who got the message instantly. "I wonder if we might talk alone."

The younger woman walked over and helped the widow sit back down. "You answer their questions, and I will go get some fresh, hot tea." With that, the girl kissed Mrs. Stellar on the head and left the room.

"Mrs. Stellar. I won't take up much of your time during this stressful period." Bower leaned forward in the chair and spoke in a low voice. He knew that a lot of women were attracted to him, and he hated to use it, but he let her look at his face and eyes. Perhaps it would let her relax.

Dabbing her eyes with a lace handkerchief, she did let out a sigh and nod. Giving her time to relax and be alone with him, he smiled. "I am so sorry for your loss, Mrs. Stellar."

"Please, call me Rose." Her smile was weak, but it was a start.

"Thank you, Rose." He gave her one of his winning smiles. It seemed to work as she leaned back in the chair and crossed her legs. "Rose, do you have any idea what your husband was doing at the Club La Masque so late last night?"

"No, I have never heard of that club. He has never taken me there. It must have been a medical emergency. Sometimes, he gets called out at all hours. He is" — she paused — "so devoted to his chosen career."

The rest of his questions did not give him as much information as she answered to his first. Just the way she answered that first question told him she did not know what type of club it was and why her husband was a patron. She did give him the name and address of her husband's best friend from the hospital. She said it was a man and that they often went on calls together and tried to find time to catch a beer together once in a while. Another name for the puzzle.

Standing up, he waved her to stay in her seat. The timing was right, as the young woman came in with a tray of what he supposed was the tea.

Rob was waiting at the door as she had been with the younger woman.

"Again, Mrs. Stellar, Rose, my condolences. Thank you for your time." He gave her a nod and turned to follow Rob and the maid out to the front door.

Waiting until they walked around to the driver's side of Rob's van where they were sheltered, Bower turned to his partner. "What did you find out?"

Nodding, Rob opened her heavier pad. "Well, it was Stellar's submissive, Dina Diarmon. Her family have been friends for years. Her dad works in administration at the hospital. I have their home address, but it is different from hers." Now, Rob had done some work on her fancy tablet before continuing. "She says she was supposed to meet him at the club later, but when she got there, the cops were everywhere. She says the wife doesn't know anything about her husband's unusual activities and that she also participated in them. She was here for mutual comfort. She didn't share her connection with the Doctor and the club."

Their next stop was on the same side of the city but not quite as expensive. It was the apartment of Bruce Archer, who worked for the legal firm where Martha Saluda was one of the leading attorneys. Mrs. Saluda was a legal official who handled divorces, especially for very hefty customers. Evidently, Mr. Archer had a well-paying position, as he lived in one of the complexes that had an underground parking lot and a beautiful lobby.

The catch was you couldn't get beyond the lobby until one of the two people, one behind a counter and the other near the front door, called up. The counterman called Mr. Archer to tell him the police needed to talk to him. After the man hung up, he came out from behind the counter and led them to a bank of elevators.

It looked to Bower that anyone could push the button, but the man made a show of hitting the up button and waited for them to enter. He then reached in and punched the number five button that lit up. The partners looked at each other, knowing that once the door was closed, that they could punch any new floor button. The show was for the security cameras, both in the lobby and in the elevator.

Meeting them at the door and inviting them into the very comfortable apartment, Brice Archer was a man in his early thirties. He was a handsome man, almost too pretty, so it made him have a soft look about his movements. But his voice was firm. "Please, have a seat, detectives." Mr. Archer seemed comfortable. "I assume you are here to ask me questions about my co-worker, Attorney Mrs. Saluda. It was a shock, and I don't know if everyone in the firm has been notified yet."

"You worked personally with Mrs. Saluda?" Rob had her tablet out to take notes.

"Somewhat. But I worked mostly with Mr. Roy Montgomery, the head Attorney." Now, his voice had turned cold.

Bower looked at him and understood this was the face that Archer showed around the office. Bower knew how to handle this situation. Standing up, without looking at his partner, he pulled out his phone and put it on record. Then, in his Dom voice, he gave an order to Rob. "Partner, step out. I will join you later."

As Rob got the message and hurried from the room, Archer also understood and slid forward on his chair, placing his hands on his knees.

"Brice, why did you not attend the club with Martha Saluda?" Bower continued to tower over the other man, who was almost as tall as he was. But the man took the instant submissive slump of his shoulders.

"I am ashamed. I didn't even know my Mistress was going to the club. I would have climbed on hands and knees to save her." Now, the tears became real ones.

"Did she go to the club often alone?" Bower let his voice be harsh and break through the sobs.

Wiping his nose with the back of his hand, the pretty man looked up. "As far as I know, we always went together. She insisted I drive."

"You were her only sub?"

Now, the man slid down on his knees and took the full plead. "Yes, she told me I was perfect. She had some before me, but she told me she gave them all up and wiped them from her memory after I came to her feet."

"What about the people at the workplace, the office? Do any of them know about your Dom's preference in nightlife?" Bower waited.

Now, the man got brave and raised his head. "No. That was a separate part of her life. There is no way she would allow her private life to interfere with her work."

Turning and leaving the man crying on his knees, Bower left, figuring he had got all there was to be had at this location. He shared the general information with Rob on the way down the elevator. They both pushed different floor buttons to drive the entry guard nuts.

Their next stop was to visit the widow of Donald Prentice. Both detectives felt it was important to get a lot of information at his home. There were so many answers waiting since Rob agreed with Bower that Donald Prentice was the real target.

CHAPTER SEVEN

Tracking down details on the internet and through the normal Police records was Rob's job. It was more difficult than she expected, which she loved and perked her excitement.

So far, it looked like all the people killed at the Club La Masque lived on the right side of the city. Part of that was probably because of the high ticket cost for membership in the club. This was a stand-alone large home along a series of avenues with several of the same high-priced residences.

There was a long, well-lit driveway that turned at the front of the two-story house. Bower noticed the security cameras in trees and on the house. If one called the tall edifice two stories, Bower had to guess that each floor had very high ceilings.

This time, they left Rob's van in a parking lot and went together in the low Interceptor. On the ride, Rob did mention some of the things she had discovered about Mrs. Prentice to her partner.

"First, she was rich before they got married and has all the money tied up in prenups and separate legal agreements. His Real Estate Investment company is barely hanging on. This house and property are entirely in her name. Now, here is the strange thing. There is a large life insurance policy on her and only one hundred thousand on him. She keeps that much in her checking account." Rob finished as the door was opened by a butler.

The man was dressed in the usual butler's outfit — white shirt, black bow tie, and matching black vest. But this man was definitely ex-military. His hair was crew cut, and even though he greeted them with a pleasant word, Bower saw how he looked them over carefully. He noted where their weapons were located and that none were in their hands.

Identifying themselves, Rob asked to talk to Mrs. Prentice concerning the death of her husband.

"Of course." The butler, who was a bodyguard, did not smile. "Please come in. I will have the maid show you to a waiting room and contact Mrs. Prentice."

A middle-aged woman who was a bit overweight stepped out of a side door. She was dressed in the standard maid's uniform, with a dress a bit long and solid shoes. Bower had one thought—the help was hired to do the job, not for their looks.

The maid led them down the wide hall, which had master-pieces hanging on the walls and several closed doors. Bower had guessed correctly about the height of the ceilings, as this was the tallest hallway he had visited.

The room she told them to make themselves comfortable in as she left was a sitting room with a fake fireplace complete with a make believe fire behind a screen. There were fancy wooden chairs with padded seats and backs that would never be comfortable. The one short couch had too many pillows. There were small rugs over the dark carpeting.

"This has to be a room that is never used by the family." Rob sniffed as she sat down in one chair and opened her large tablet on her knees. They were made to wait for at least fifteen minutes, and Bower never took a seat and didn't pace. He just stood calmly behind one of the other chairs. They had both played this game before when talking to politicians, officials, and other wealthy people.

It was obvious the maid was holding the door for the lady who entered.

Bower looked at her closely as she walked in with her head

high.

She went over and sat in the center of the couch. She was either in her early forties or someone older who had the money to appear younger. "I will give you one-half hour, and then all further questions and time will be through my attorneys." Margaret Prentice spoke, looking up at Bower and ignoring Rob.

Since she had chosen sharpness, Bower decided to skip any remorse and go directly to pertinent questions. "Did you know your husband intended to go the Club La Masque two nights ago?"

She didn't even flinch. "We had different night lives. I had no knowledge of anything or where he went after his work hours. We sometimes attended functions together, but that was the limit of our social time together."

Looking over at Rob, who was making some notes, she was staying quiet and letting him handle the powerful widow. Bower did not move as he continued. "Was there a divorce in the plans?"

Now, Mrs. Prentice looked at her fingernails as if making sure her appearance was perfect. "Why would either of us suffer the embarrassment of such an action?" Now, she raised her eyes to glare at Bower.

This was one time when he realized his good looks were a handicap. This woman found a handsome policeman distasteful. It did not fit in her world of people who were below her and should fall into their places.

Smoothly, the lady stood up. "I think this conversation is done. I will have my butler give you a card from my attorney's office. Please do not return here without a warrant. Thank you." With that, she nodded and walked past them, as she reached the door, it opened. The maid was waiting with a hand on a door knob.

Bower decided the maid had an ear against the door to hear

when the boss was ready to leave a room. But the maid did wait for them, and when Rob got up, she led them back out to the front door. Sure enough, the Special Ops butler handed Rob a business card and stood in the open door to watch them drive away.

Smiling at Rob, Bower made a remark. "A real friendly group."

"Yep." Rob put away her tablet. "No wonder the husband sought outside fun."

"Well, we are going to have some more fun. There is Donald Prentice's Dom, the guy that put him on the cross." Bower was driving to take Rob back to her van.

"That is a problem." Rob tapped her closed tablet. "The guy is missing." Now, she opened the metal-enclosed tablet and quickly swiped up some information. "His name is Richard Carrier or commonly known as Dick. Not at his apartment. They got the apartment manager to let them in for a health check, and it looked like he had never returned from the night of the murder. The Captain has black-and-whites outside the complex. But so far, there has not been a missing person filed."

They returned to the Precinct to spend some time on the Police system chasing down information. Bower was looking for all the latest RE deals and contracts that Prentice had been involved in to get a list of additional people to interrogate.

The job for Rob was to chase down family and friends and where Richard Carrier worked. His family, which was only one parent and some cousins, were out of state, and he had not visited them for some time. He worked in management in a small office that ran local fast-food restaurants.

There were only twelve people in that office, and it closed every day at six in the evening. There was almost no weekend work, so Mr. Carrier had a lot of free time. But it was not a high-paying job, so how did he handle the fee at Club La Masque?

After going to fill his large mug of coffee, Bower walked across to the Geek Section. He was hoping they had found some scenes of Carrier coming and going at the Club.

Unfortunately, the young people in this division, with their multi keyboards, earbuds, and several screens, had too many questions for him. The Club and the kink sex was a bit new and hard to understand for someone who lived within safe worlds.

The question that came up and had eyes staring at him was about the safe word. It was hard for these kids, some who didn't even watch porn, to understand that people could accept pain and humiliation as part of love and sex.

In exchange with the education he was giving as he answered the many naïve questions, he got some pics of Carrier and his car along with a shot of him leaving his apartment and not taking his car. There had to be a taxi somewhere that picked him up, so the Geek Squad went on a cab hunt.

An hour of comparing notes with his partner meant that Bower was ready for more coffee after the restroom. By the time he got back to the shared double cubby, Rob was gone, but one of the techs, a girl, was waiting. She was dressed in torn jeans and a too big sweat shirt with the name of a north eastern college. For some reason, most of the electronic pursuers got their final years in that area. She had wild-streaked hair and a contact of some kind in one ear. These people seemed to be plugged in all the time.

"Detective, we found the cab you were looking for." She held out prints of photos of cabs and then a printed sheet with all the information on the taxi, driver, and company.

"Great, these companies are open all night, so my partner and I can stop tonight." He turned to take a seat, but the girl didn't leave. "Is there something else?"

"Well, um." The girl shifted from one foot to another and then looked over her shoulder. They were too far away across the large room to see the activity in her area, where everyone was sitting down behind banks of screens. "There are a couple of bets going on among us over there." She tossed her head in what he guessed was across the area.

"Sure, what is it?" Bower turned in his chair to face her.

Rob returned, taking her seat and ignoring the girl talking.

"Don't pay any attention to my partner. Believe me, as my partner, she has seen it all."

"See, it's about the so called safe word. Can it be used any time?" Now, the girl glanced over at Rob. "Can it be used anytime, like if the girl doesn't feel like a kiss?"

"First of all, you have to understand the relationship." Now, Bower looked up to get the girl's full attention. "It is a relationship, not a quick date. You wouldn't have sex on the first time you met someone, it takes time to know them and like them as a person. In the partnership of Dom and sub, that takes a while."

Now, the girl was listening as if taking notes and finally understanding, so Bower continued. "I guess sometimes you might meet someone and are attracted to them immediately. Talking to them for a few minutes, you find out you like the same type of movies or" — he pointed to her ear attachment — "you might both find you prefer the same type of equipment. Well, that can happen in the world of BDSM. A lot of times, a sub and Dom are drawn together." He shrugged and decided he had said enough. There was so much more this innocent would not understand. "I think that's enough. We both need to get back to work. Thanks for the info." Bower turned and picked up the printouts she had brought to him.

"Well, detective. There is the bet." She put her hands together as is pleading.

Now, both Bower and Rob looked at her.

"Okay," Bower asked with a sigh, wanting to get back to work. "What is it?"

Now, the girl backed up and looked around as if she was looking for a way to escape. "When you participated, were you a Dom or a sub?"

Handsome Reed Bower, who stood six feet two inches tall, had thick dark hair and, blue eyes and shoulders to fill out his leather coat, let out a laugh that could be heard across two aisles.

It was his partner, Rob, who also spoke through her laughter to answer the girl. "Dom. Are you willing to find out more?"

Now, the girl did turn and began to run between cubbies and down different aisles until she disappeared across the room.

Chapter Eight

Both detectives, having had their fill of education from the computer and electronics division, were back on the road. Their goal was the cab company. The one good thing about taxis was that the state, and this city required good records, both from each driver and at the company's offices.

What they had was a photo of the cab's ID number that was painted large on the side. There was also the smaller company name under the number.

Parking his low-slung Mustang behind his partner's van on the street, they entered the garage with the standard office in the center. Each shift manager wanted to be able to see in all directions, so this center's small open building was an owner's pride. The counters extended out on all four sides so that whoever approached from any side could lean and wait.

There were two side exits, and the shift manager was inside on a computer when they stopped and showed their badges. This guy was one hundred percent up to date and either liked working with cops or knew they were all under many cameras. After all, a lot of money went in and out of this area.

This company had a system. The drivers put all cash and reports into a money bag that was given to them at the start of their shift. When they returned, the bag was dropped into a large metal container that looked like a bank vault. The credit card information was automatically downloaded on each hit back to the central office.

Once daily, on the day shift, a Brinks truck with armed guards came and unloaded the drop box. The funds were counted somewhere else. Discrepancy problems were sent to the proper shift manager through the computer with details, and they were told to talk to the driver. It was very efficient, and the only police calls were for a couple of fights.

This manager was loaded with work but also respected the badges when the detectives presented them. "You have my full attention," the short man said as he handed what looked like a blue bank bag to a driver on the other side.

"We need the information on this cab at this time." Rob slid the photo of the cab over to the manager. It showed the number, and at the bottom was the date and time.

"It will take me a minute to pull this up." He turned, hit a couple of buttons, grabbed another blue bag, and stuck a clipboard in front of another driver. The driver signed and disappeared with the bag. This busy manager could handle more than one thing at a time, as Bower heard a printer under the counter working.

With a swift motion, the busy man reached down and tore off a sheet that he examined before passing it over. This was the type of paper that had feed holes in the sides and was perforated every eleven inches. That meant there was probably a large container below the printer to constantly feed the machine.

Laying the sheet down under the lights from above the office over each side counter, both detectives read the information. It gave the times and mileage of the route the taxi had performed on a trip before the designated time, one they needed, and one after that time. The manager was being careful.

"Sir, what does this mileage indicate as a location for the taxi on that date and time?" Rob asked loud enough to be heard over the cars that were coming and going, mostly going.

The manager turned and ignored the driver on the

opposite side. "I don't have to look." He waved away the paper that Rob started to hold up for him. "That was an airport run. Our guys love those because they get the pay for the long run out, and there is always a paid run waiting at the airport to come back into the city. That is what the next time info is about."

"Thank you for your time," Rob announced loudly as the man turned away to take care of the waiting and impatient driver. There was no response from the busy man.

Now, Rob would spend some time on her special tablet checking flights for Richard Carrier's ticket. If he used a different name, they would need a warrant to get airport camera footage. The cameras at the airport were good, especially at the gates for boarding.

Standing at the back open doors of his partner's van, Bower had a strange thought. The kind that one who had been a member of the BDSM might be the only one to think about. "Rob, can you bring up the shots forensic took of the murder shots where everyone is still in place?"

"Sure." Rob already had her large tablet online and hit a few keys. "I keep everything in separate folders."

Being efficient, she had the photos open and the screen divided into four sections. There was a shot of Dr. Stellar in the reception lobby. But the other three were one of Prentice on the cross, another of Saluda on the floor, and the last was a full shot of that room showing both bodies.

Now Bower sighed. "Where are their masks?"

Rob zoomed in on the shots, enlarging the floor around the cross at Prentice's feet and then doing the same around Saluda's body. There were few marks in her blood, but none of the kind that would be the missing mask.

"Maybe they didn't wear them that night," Rob muttered as she changed the views.

"Detective Pervis, the club is called Club La Masque for a

reason." Bower used her title to get her attention.

"Damn, did the killer have the time to take the masks as souvenirs?" Now Rob was full into the blow-ups of the photos.

"Well, we need to check with the morgue and see if Dr. Stellar's mask is still with his clothes. After all, he wasn't officially inside the club." He had quit looking at the photos, knowing Rob was not going to find the missing masks.

"That should already be on a list. Let me see if I can pull it up." Rob's fingers danced over the screen, signing into police records using her ID.

"We're also going to have to do some research to find what the masks look like for Prentice and Saluda." Bower was thinking out loud.

Looking over at her partner with her eyebrows raised, Rob had to ask. "Are you saying that a mask is not just a mask? That these people might have different and distinct masks?" She had to shake her head. She was learning too much about the odd habits of what she assumed were normal people. These people were out in the real world as a doctor, a divorce attorney and a real estate investor. Someone you would see in everyday life that led to a different personality at night.

Taking her gaze off her partner, she realized that even a policeman had been in that confusing life. He had left it and found it not for him, but it pointed out to her that she would never be able to guess who led what she had thought was a normal life.

"Okay, partner. I have to ask. Did you ever wear a mask?" Rob turned from the gruesome photos to look up at Bower to see his reaction.

As usual, he showed nothing, but he answered. "I did not belong to Club La Masque. But there was one I wore for a special request and show. It was a fitted leather eye mask with no decorations. Now put your curiosity away, and what did you find out about the good doctor's mask?"

On her screen, she had a notice in her Dropbox, and it was an answer from the morgue. Opening the report, it was a complete list of everything on Dr. Frank Stellar as found at time of demise. The list included sock color and receipts, an amount of cash, and several thousand. Yes, there was a mask, and the report included a small photo.

"Partner." Rob was trying to blow up the rough photo of the mask. "Is that some kind of jewels on the front side of the doctor's mask?"

"Probably. Most Doms have their masks decorated. The personal mask is also made to order to fit the face, so it is expensive and not sold in front of the Extreme Items stores." In his mind, Bower was pretty much eliminating Stellar as being connected to the murder. Collateral damage was part of a lot of crimes.

But the big problem now was the two missing masks. There was no way Saluda would be in that club without hers on, and whoever put Prentice up on the cross would not remove his mask in this room. With no cameras within this organization and Bower knew these two people would never wear their covers outside, he put to the top of the puzzle list to find the description of the two missing masks.

Feeling frustrated, Bower left his partner and returned to his car. It seemed like his crossword puzzle was getting bigger in this chase for the unknown killer. But at last, before either of them could decide where to go next on this full shift, they got a message. There was a trace on the weapon.

CHAPTER NINE

Sometimes, a weapon can't be traced, but bullets can. The well-organized, methodical killer had left unshot bullets in the gun. He was too well-planned and logical to handle anything without gloves. But someone else had left fingerprints on the unspent cartridges. That would be the person who had either the bullets or the weapon before the perp.

By the time Bower pulled into the Reserved parking place that was not for him, behind the main police station, he was getting notices from the Electronics Division.

Instead of going to that department, he went to his desk within the double cubby and opened the attached screen. Two different identifiable prints were on the four unspent bullets. The nerd crew had done their job and produced a Driver's License that showed the bad photos, but there was more.

There were last known addresses of the two individuals, and one of them was in the local jail. He had been caught on an outstanding warrant and went right to the city prison for four years. Bower would start with him, as he was easy to find.

The main long-term jail was two blocks over toward what was termed the wrong side of town. Surprisingly, there was no crime, due to the large walls of the prison and the presence of so many cops, officials, and family visitors. On one street were two multi-story garages.

There were entrances on all four sides of the prison, but that was a trick because there was only one place inside that led to the inner cells. Bower knew which entrance would get him into the interview section, so he parked on the street next to a door. He put his police notice in the front window and went inside the large, cold building.

Knowing the routine, Bower helped himself to coffee as he signed the proper papers and emptied his pockets. He took off the ankle backup, the big Magnum, and even his watch. The metal detectors at this modern holding system were top-drawer. He had even seen some cops who had to go through a body search for extra forgotten metal trinkets.

It took him as long to reclaim all of his items afterward while he tucked the small thirty-eight into the ankle holster. The cop attendants were admiring the large Magnum but were smart enough not to touch it.

Change, trinkets, a watch, and his baby tucked into its special place near his back so a bulge wouldn't show, he double-checked the wooden box and nodded. He might need to see this team again, so it never paid to make enemies. A friendly smile was returned as he went through two more doors and into the standard visiting area for accused and sentenced persons.

He had been told that seat three would be where the prisoner would soon be escorted out. Bower took the chair and waited, finishing off his coffee. The boys in charge didn't make him wait too long. The slam of the metal door that slid sideways announced the prisoner and one guard.

In this modern facility, all the doors moved sideways. This made it easier to lock everything down and prevent a guard from being slammed by a door. Also, since most of the doors were heavy metal, they could be moved without power, but not very fast. With power and under the control of guards protected in control towers, any door rolled open smoothly. The backup power for this large building was redundant.

The young black man took a seat across from Bower on an identical seat. The counter seemed to be the same as if it stretched from one to the other about six feet across. Although Bower had heard the sound of the metal door, probably resounding through the floor, he could not hear what the guard said to Mathia Acto Roundtree.

Having read his sheet before requesting the visit, Bower already knew he was dealing with a stupid street product. This thirty-eight-year-old man probably had more friends behind bars than he did outside.

Picking up the phone, which was the only way to talk, Bower stared through the thick, unbreakable plexiglass that separated them. Halfway between them on their shared counter, the special clear unit was inserted down and capped above by a wall. This was to prevent the passing of any contraband to inmates.

Finally, Mathia, known among some recently as Post, reached for the phone. It was out of curiosity and a way to stay out of the cell block for a while. He would probably tell some made-up story of what happened when he was gone.

"Wha' tha' fuck ya' want an who tha' fuck is yo'?" Yep, Mathia had also been educated on the streets.

"I'm Detective Bower of the Homicide Division. Mathia, at a murder scene, we found a gun, and it had a bullet with your fingerprint on it." Now Bower tried his best smile, looking like the cat who ate the cream.

"I don't kill no fuckin' no one. Call me Post." At least now Bower had the jerk's full attention.

"Hey, Post. The proof is what put you in this place, and the proof of a thumb and fingerprint on a bullet will send you to the chair."

"Naw, no, naw. Ya got the wrong fuckin' guy. Who got knocked and when?" Post was gripping the large single phone piece, and his bones were showing white through his black knuckles.

"Donald Prentice, the Real Estate investor. He was a really

rich guy, and someone wanted him dead." Bower watched the man through the clear window as Post tried to remember everything he had done that might have led up to killing someone.

"Yeah, you fuckin' cops are all dumb. I don' know no real estate whats about. Oh, I sold ta' gun an all, that be it, fuckin' asshole. I sold the fuckin' gun, and I was locked up?" Post looked hopeful.

"Post, I never said what gun I was talking about. What are you talking about?"

Now the rat brain smarts set in, and Post shook his head but didn't say anything.

"Post, I already have the results of the fingerprints, and they have put together with you. They are going to check every camera in this place, and each time, you weren't seen even when you took a piss. Now, when was the last time you had a gun? What was it, and who has it? That might save your skin." Now, he had the rat's attention.

For the next half hour that was left of his time with the visit with a prisoner, the rat squealed. He not only told who he got the gun from in a trade but also the name, address, and street gang friends of the next punk to hold the forty-five.

That meant that when Bower left the hallways with a big thank you to the guards, he had his next destination. He did sit in the comfortable car to catch up on his notes and talk to Rob, giving her the details he had obtained. Naturally, she worked her larger, efficient tablet and soon sent him a mugshot and copy of an expired Driver's License of Efrin Thomas Belfran, aka Boot.

Both detectives knew that the street names Post and Boot were common and used more than once among different gangs or toughs who worked the streets. Boot was a bit younger than Post, with long braided locks, some of which were his own hair. His skin tone was a bit lighter, so mixed blood was in his family line.

Boot's sheet proved that he lived on the streets as his first real trouble started with a knife fight at school at twelve. Sent to reform school, he was out and on the street at sixteen with an education he got not from teachers but from the other kids. The jails were swinging doors for this addict who stole anything to support his habit.

Unfortunately, Boot was out in the hood and not at the address he gave to his parole officer. In fact, no one had seen him at that address or anywhere else. Right now, he was a street shadow, which was common with many men without jobs, but he needed to get a fix.

None of Bower's or Rob's contacts claimed that they either didn't know Boot or hadn't seen him in weeks. Both detectives spread some cash around with promise of more for information. All they could do now was wait and post a Need Notice among all the black-and-whites. Doing some driving and catching food on the go, the shift was soon over. It was time to head for the bed for both of them.

Going by the Precinct, not to go up and into work, but to run the Mustang Interceptor through the car wash in the back of the garage and fill it up on the high octane they kept for all the cop cars. Bower liked the car wash because it used long ribbons of cloth and no rolling brushes.

One last stop at a place that opened up early with strong coffee, he took the jumbo-size home with him. Another night was gone, and these two busy detectives, dedicated to their jobs, could not even remember if they had a shift off or not.

The next few shifts, including a weekend, Bower spent on the street, except when he and his partner went to the hospital where Dr. Stellar had worked. They also visited the office Prentice occupied in a large upscale building in the middle of the finance center.

They got more questions about the La Masque club and what type of sex was supposed to be part of its life from the shocked workers. There was little information except what nice guys both men were, and no one would have guessed they belonged to such an organization.

As usual, Rob smiled as a lot of ladies wanted to flirt with her handsome partner. A couple of times, he used that smile to get some extra papers or information. For Rob, whatever worked to get data for her tablet was great.

On a late-night shift, with Rob in the office and Bower looking at Saluda's building, there was a special notice. It seemed that there was an acknowledgment of a Person of Interest report. Their dear friend Mr. Boot had been picked up on a minor drug bust, and a sharp intake cop had checked the sheets before letting him out on the usual one thousand bail. They were holding him at a small local intake Police Department.

Sending through a compliment to the duty officer, Bower requested that Efrin Thomas Belfran, aka Boot, be transferred to the main Precinct. Bower knew that at his home location, he could talk to Boot in an interrogation room for as long as it took to get the details on the forty-five.

Going on into the attorney's building to talk to the cleaning help, he spent some time finding who cleaned the halls and who handled emptying the big bins where the drop chutes dropped down to the basement. He got an education.

First, the crew in the basement was more than willing to talk about what came down the chutes. They told him of new shoes, whole bags of groceries, and more bedclothes than needed to fill up a hotel. They all stated they were afraid of the bottles of drugs and were glad to dress up in safety gear when items with blood appeared. Most of the time, they sifted through for landfill or burnable items.

The problem for these workers was that the owners

expected a lot of stuff to be used in the large furnaces for power. Anything that was safe to burn was a power source and free if it came down the chutes. But they assured him nothing came down from the legal offices. There was a special truck that came to the back entrance once a month and accepted all bags of shredded paper. They also did their type of shredding, the kind that left small chips, not long strips. Someone paid a lot for that secure disposal of trash.

One last chat with the doorman and Bower headed back to Precinct Thirty-Three. He figured he had allowed enough for the transfer work and the actual movement of Boot. Now, he had a hope to be one step closer to the BDSM killer.

Chapter Ten

W hile still driving, Bower called in a request for Boot to be put into an interrogation room. One stop to get a jumbo black extra strong coffee, then he was soon going through what was almost a tunnel to the area where the holding area was located.

With a big smile and a thank you to the woman who was on duty, he signed the sheet and proceeded to the room she told him was where his man was waiting.

"Care if I watch?" She indicated a batch of computer screens all lit up. "It has been a boring night."

"Hey, help yourself. I promise not to beat him up too much." Bower winked at her and walked down the hall with her laughter.

The room had the occupied light on, and he stopped and put the big Magnum into the box beside the door, taking the key for it and dropping the key into a pocket. He ignored the small thirty-eight in the ankle holster, not because he was worried about Boots, but because he never went naked.

The man was a bit younger than the previous gun owner, but he had been beaten up by the streets and drugs. His face and arms were pockmarked, and he probably had never been a nice-looking person. Sitting in the usual position, facing the window and armed with handcuffs locked to the table.

This meant that Bower came into his side and jerked his head as if expecting to be stuck. Walking around the table, Bower pulled out the chair that put his back to the dark one-way window and sat down. At this point, Bower didn't think anyone was watching in the other room as most people were gone, considering the hour, although he did know the bored guard up front was watching through the recording camera. In this city, all interviews were recorded. They were stored on discs that took up less room and lasted forever.

Opening his long leather jacket, Bower leaned back and waited. He had not brought the usual folder to lay on the table and didn't say anything. He only looked at the man whose gaze was going everywhere but not directly at him. His purpose was to make the street hood uncomfortable and afraid, so he believed whatever the man in charge said.

It didn't take long for Boot to start to shift in the chair and look at the door as if hoping someone else would come in. At last, he couldn't take it.

"Wha' ta' fuck ya' lookin' at?" His voice changed as he swallowed.

"A dead man," Bower said the words calmly but firmly.

Now, the man looked around at the room and the black window. "Ya' think ya' can kill me here an' get away wit' it?"

What happened through the next couple of hours was that Efrin Thomas Belfran, aka Boot, said too much. The sale of the forty-five that he obtained in a trade for drugs was the biggest score he had capped. In this addict's mind, a stupid whitie had laid down five hundred cold ones for the piece.

As the interrogator, Bower had a problem keeping the addled mind on the subject. Boot wandered off on anything that caught his attention. When he told about the first contact on a bud's throwaway, he immediately went off on a tangent of how many contacts that gang had, and they could bust him and get a shit load of info.

If Bower mentioned the death at the sex club, Boot's rattled on about a whole lot of free sex on the two block area where he bought his hits. It took all his will not to tie Boot down and gag him. But some of the words were useful.

The street bum talked about the drawer he found at a house where a bunch of users hung out to sleep off and not get mugged. In the drawer were all type of bullets. It took Boot twenty minutes to explain how he tried out different shells to get a couple more into the clip. Except Boot called it the bullet holder thing.

At last, they got around to describing the buyer.

"Ya' know. All whities look alike." Boot shrugged.

"Did he look like me? Do my eyes look the same color as his?" Now Bower leaned forward and put some deep tone in his voice.

"Naw wasn't as pretty. Had dark eyes like us niggers."

"Good." Pulling details from Boot about the buyer would have been easier than if he had been pulling some teeth with a pair of pliers. "Okay, and was his hair light in color like mine?" The room was bright with all the lights on as Bower had wanted the prisoner to see him.

"Nope, ya' folks are all different and strange."

"Sure, but his hair color was about the color of my leather coat?"

"That's a fine jacket. I cod' a use one like it." Now Boot licked his lips.

"We have a bargain. I will give you this one when I leave if you help me decide how the gun buyer looks. Now what that is on me or in this room matches the color of his hair?" Bower began to push the leather coat off.

"Yo' shirt."

The shirt the detective had on was a washed out standard brown cotton with a collar and a couple buttons but generally a pull over. It was a light brown or tan. Now Bower stood up, leaving the long jacket on the chair.

"Was he as tall as me?"

"Whoa." Boot looked around. "Uh, yo a big gun. Can you stand by me?"

Walking around the metal bolted-down table, Bower waited for Boot to stand. Boot was limited by the handcuffs attached to the table but could rise to full height. The punk was only five feet eight inches and hardly came up to the detective's shoulder.

"He wooda' come to yo' ear." Boot said as he sat back down.

The next discussion about whether the man was fat or thin went off on another tangent, suggesting that all whities were fat. It took an effort for the detective to get from Boot that the man matched the size of his cousin Matcho.

At last, Bower left without his coat and the need to locate a new street addict with the punk name of Matcho. He would put the cost of a new coat on his department expense report and sent to his partner Rob to trace down a local street black called Matcho. He knew she would use her remarkable large tablet and also put in a note to the nerd department.

With a look at the fancy reports that Rob had put together, he spent some time in his car, eating a meal and composing a note to Captain Martin. He always had to show the boss that they had been working before asking for something.

What he was asking for was a warrant for the La Masque club for the list of memberships. Bower had a hunch that the killer was a member and had been in the club many times, enough to be totally familiar with the layout.

After spending the rest of his shift traveling the streets, answering one call as a backup, and filling in his puzzle, he contacted Rob to tell her he was calling it a night.

The next night, as he ate breakfast, he was pleasantly surprised with a lot of messages on what the Precinct was calling the Sex Murders. Rob had full details on Matcho, and he was local and still on the streets. Rob had included several mug shots but never had a driver's license. The most recent photo in front of the lines showed him five feet nine inches and a standard black man. He had his hair short but in fancy tight braids across his head.

The second important note was from the aide to the boss telling him there was a completed warrant in his office mailbox. It meant he had to go by the Precinct, but that was okay as he could check with the computer group for general activity.

But first, before the store closed, he needed to go by his favorite men's shop and get a new leather coat. He was a big man and often found it difficult to find clothes to fit. But for the right price, at this one shop, they had what he needed. It wouldn't take long, and he paid in cash and kept the receipt for his expense report. There was nothing like the smell of a new leather coat, so he almost thanked Boot for the trade of a jacket for a description of what he hoped the guys and gals in electronics could use to build up a face and description from what an addict said.

The large and busy electronics division had a dozen questions that Bower dodged, and the younger ones asked about submission. It seemed it was easy to find any type of porn, including some really ugly types on the internet and the dark net. However, they found that the group of BDSM was camera shy. The clubs forbade cameras and cell phones and made heavy provisions to prevent anything from being taken in, even the new tiny watch and button recording devices.

One of the newbies asked Bower how the club owners kept out the small new vids.

Accepting printouts, he wanted to keep on this group's good side, so he decided to take a moment for explanations. After all, he was the only cop they knew about who had gone undercover to the strange scene.

"Well, guys." Bower gave one of his famous white teeth smiles that brought a bump to a couple of hearts. "First of all, these clubs are floating in money. It is in their best interest to keep up to the latest inventions. They have on their payrolls hackers, not on site, but good ones who are paid to keep up with the latest products and techniques, including the military and our friends the Chinese."

There were a couple of "Wows" heard, and quite a few leaned forward to catch every word, which was the rare item not on their fancy machines.

"Anyone going into a club either leaves their equipment and watches at home or in the car. There is a security lock box provided for each person who enters a club to lock their items until they leave." That reminded him that he needed another warrant for the lock boxes at the La Masque club. He mentally kicked himself as if he had not thought of the boxes before.

Seeing all the questioning faces, he decided to wrap it up, so he waved the printouts. "There is one new modern device added to clubs. When the person goes through the final hall to enter the main room, of course, it is a metal detector, just like the airport. But there is also a burst of EMP. Bingo, all devices are burnt. No button camera will function. Thanks for the image."

Stopping for a moment at his desk, he sent a request for the contents of the private lock boxes at the club. This was an open request, and the boxes would be opened by a police security force under supervision. All contents would be secured and brought back to the evidence room at the Precinct house in a special section that held suspect material. Since the items were connected with a murder case, they would be isolated and stored where the general police population did not have availability.

Next, he examined the drawing of a man that Matcho described.

CHAPTER ELEVEN

Looking at the printouts, there was a general computer or artist drawing of a face of a Caucasian man with light brown hair and dark eyes. Based on the recordings that the computer teams listened to from Matcho, they developed a man in late thirties with deep frown lines.

With the standard police marks, it was indicated that he was five foot eleven inches tall, in shape but not muscular. Bower smiled, thinking the man was probably a rock wall climber at the gym and not a wrestler.

The last thing he needed was to swing by the wall of open mailboxes to pick up the warrant he and Rob could serve at the sex club to get into their membership list. That was going to cause a whole shitload of problems that he and Rob were the type to handle.

They met and parked in the side parking lot that had the police tape now on the ground. But there were still large orange warning letters taped to the doors and walls. There was one car in the lot, a nice new Cadillac sedan. Someone still appreciated American labor.

The side door was locked, so they went around to the front and now had to sign on a sheet with a street cop who had duty inside the lobby. They made their way through what was a very clean building with everything shut down except for night lights and red exit signs.

They didn't bother to knock as they entered the office, and the woman who owned and ran this shop jerked up with a frown. Still, Joella Margret Reviv was under control and didn't rise or call out. This woman felt she could be in command and control of any situation.

Indicating to Rob not to sit, Bower approached the desk and slammed the warrant down in front of the owner. "Mrs. Reviv, this is a warrant signed by the Chief of the Supreme Court to immediately obtain a copy of all membership lists to this club."

Knowing that calling her Mrs. instead of Mistress irritated her, and the fact that they were standing while addressing her left her at a disadvantage.

There was the wait while Mrs. Reviv called her lawyer and another long time until the lawyer and an assistant arrived almost an hour later. Evidently, the lawyer's office wasn't open this late at night, but he did respond to his well-paying clients.

Next, they all sat down when extra chairs were brought in by a cleaning lady while the lawyer and the pretty assistant went carefully through the five-page warrant.

"Well, detectives, this all seems to be in order. When do you expect to pick up the paperwork?" The attorney looked sad as he was probably finding a fee slipping away from one of his pockets.

"We need it now, so we can wait." Bower made his voice firm. To confirm the statement, Rob set her metal-encased tablet on the desk and attached a cord.

"I can attach direct to your system and download anything that is available." Rob let a loud ping come out from her unit, which was usually very quiet.

He didn't smile, but he liked working with this feisty detective.

Now, there was another argument between Joella and her attorney. Bower moved over to lean against the closed door, and Rob played on her computer.

At last, with Joella stalking out of the room and the

attorney's assistant overseeing the process, Rob was able to get a recent copy of the membership, confirmed by payment receipts. The yearly fee of ten thousand dollars for membership was just the tip of the iceberg for the money that flowed into the club.

Nothing was free inside the doors of this place of unusual sex for adults. The bar tab was high, the rent of equipment was outrageous, and to pay to have a special sub provided was unbelievable.

Rob had a dozen questions but hesitated with the attorney in the room.

At last, the attorney decided he needed to go out and find his client.

After finishing her soda, the assistant excused herself to use the connected bathroom.

Now Rob leaned back and brought up her *stickies* to make some notes. "Partner," she called attention to the tall man. "There are a lot of additional accounts here that bring in big money for the club, but the names don't make any sense. Are they selling drugs or something else illegal?"

"Usually, these clubs make a lot of cash in the legal ways." Bower leaned over the desk. "What are the titles on some of the big ones?"

"Well, there is Unique Trial. It has deposits made almost every night in large amounts." Now, she brought up the item on her screen to highlight some of the numbers.

Shaking his head, Bower sat down. "It is a term for special action. It means a request for personal humiliation. It was what the action for Prentice or his Dom paid for the use of the room and the products to put him on the cross. Under what we saw, Prentice probably paid the tab. A member can keep a running bill, like at a restaurant or a bar, and settle up nightly or at the end of the month."

There was a sigh from Rob as she brought up another large

figure. "So, what is Required Discord? I am almost afraid to ask about this one."

Bower chuckled and answered. "Oh, you would love it. That means anything regarding a whipping. It will vary depending on the product, the demand, and the pain involved. Leave it to your imagination."

There was silence, and Rob was not even making notes. That was her usual task. Bower knew she was thinking the whole picture over. The thought of Dom and sub was so alien to people who had found a normal, deep love life that it was hard to digest and understand.

For people like Detective Roberta Pervis and her husband and family, to think of humiliation and pain with the act of sex was close to sadism. But Rob was being distracted by the numbers that were coming up with the list of paid members.

"Partner, there are over two hundred names on this paid register. Do you realize how much money that means they make a year?" Rob's eyes were expanded.

"I would guess over two million." Bower's voice was non-committal.

"Did you ever have to pay a membership somewhere?" Rob asked, knowing the average pay for a detective. She supposed with some savings, a cop could pay out ten thousand for something important, but what about all the extras in the clubs?

"There are slaves and adepts who don't have to pay to be at any club or private activity, depending on their status and looks." The voice was Joella, standing in the doorway. There was no telling how long she had been there and listening.

Since Rob was sitting at the end of the desk and the attorney's assistant had a stool beside her, Joella walked around Bower, going back to her seat. As she passed him, she ran her fingers of one hand across him and smiled until she reached her chair. "One guess which one your partner is when he wears the leather."

The owner of the club, having his attention, brought to mind a question that Bower decided needed to be asked. "Mrs. Reviv, where was your sub the night of the murder?"

Taking a moment to settle into her fancy chair and turn to face everyone, the club owner finally answered, "At my home, tied to my bed where he was waiting." Her gaze was on Rob to see if there would be a reaction to her words, but Rob was deep into the computer work and disappointed her.

With both detectives getting all types of notices on their phones and computers that they were ignoring, they realized that the hours spent at the office of the club owner had to end.

It was out in the parking lot when Rob stopped her partner to talk about the last conversation he had with the club owner. "Reed, she offered you to be a part owner in the club. That had to be worth millions. Then she offered you a hundred thousand cash for one appearance, whatever that means. On our civil servant's money, that is pretty beyond reach. What are you doing out here on the streets?"

Moving her away, he forced the low door open and winked at his friend and fellow detective. "Putting people like her behind bars. Believe me, one day, she will go beyond the line, and that expensive attorney will run."

With a sigh, Rob turned to get into her van. She would be glad when this case was solved and closed, and they were back to the same old crook-kills-crook.

But before they pulled out on the street, Bower stopped beside her, and with windows open, Rob looked down into the impressive low ride.

"Rob, the killer was a regular at the club. He knew the place well and was also recognized by Dr. Stellar. That is the only reason Stellar was killed. Saluda also recognized him and found an illegal hidden gun to fight back. But where the hell did she get the weapon? I also don't believe Mrs. Reviv's story about where her sub was staying on the night of the murder. But this was not the act of a sub. It was an assassination." Bower nodded and drove away. He had given his partner enough to chew on.

Working back in the office at the Precinct, Bower wondered if this was going to be one of those strange cases that got away. Would it be another box in the Cold Case department?

No, he was determined to find this killer. Finishing the night by checking on blank leads and frustrated information.

They started out their next shift early and went by the office to pick up a handful of warrants.

There was one for Mr. Dorrance W. Snyder at an apartment in the older part of the city. A team of regular police led by a forensic supervisor went to shake the place, and their first report was it seemed the man did not live at the address. There were no clothes in any of the closets or the drawers. The kitchen was bare except for some spoilt milk in the fridge. The only mail that was piled on the floor inside the door drop was all advertisements. Snyder may pay the rent at this address, reported the Supervisor, but he never spent a night in the bed with no sheets or covers.

It was Detectives' Bower and Pervis that led the large team to serve the search warrant on the mansion of Joella Margret Reviv. Joella chose to be on Bower's heels as he searched the downstairs office and library with two officers. They put items in evidence bags that all of them found suspicious, as everything was handled with gloves.

The first report from Rob was that there was no sign of Mr. Snyder, but it was evident he occupied a suite of rooms in the large home, which still had other rooms for guests, all on the second floor. At the end of the hall, there was the suite that belonged to the owner.

This was not a pleasant search for the owner, as mattresses were turned over, books were removed, and any furniture or articles against the walls were pulled away. Vent covers were opened, and some things were found. Rugs were rolled up, and ladders were brought to examine ceilings and high-solid items.

After hours in the large old house, they requested additional help. They had one police van full of leather equipment, including handcuffs, whips, leg cuffs, leg spreaders, and any imaginable leather belts for different parts of the body.

The real problem was the additional hidden access places built into the huge mansion. Some had been developed years ago when the large old home was originally built, and others had been added with great imagination. There were tunnels, crawl spaces between the walls, and closets or alcoves that only hid a person or items but went nowhere.

With all Mrs. Reviv's protesting, the problems became greater when her attorney showed up with several assistants or legal advisors. Eventually, she was advised by her attorney to leave the property, for her health and peace of mind. This was after she threw a screaming match as unusual underwear was being pulled from a hidden set of drawers from a stairway.

It was one of several sets of wide steps leading down to the basement. By accident, an investigator tripped, almost fell, and threw his weight with one arm against the side wall. A drawer that looked like a cement block popped out. There were seven of the blocks disguised as drawers, and they were very clean and full of neatly folded items that most police admitted they had never seen.

Police who saw drunks pissing on corners and dead prostitutes in alleys admit to their team that they were shocked and surprised?

CHAPTER TWELVE

To the tired search group, the night lasted until dawn, and two large haul trucks were brought in under security to remove all the paperwork and articles. Now, back in a separate garage and office, teams of forensic specialists who studied paperwork and piecework had their jobs cut out for them. There was enough for the electronics group to delve into the three computers to keep the kids happy for the next week.

In the meantime, after a good night's rest, Bower had one thing he had not turned in. It was a large photo of Dorrance W. Snyder, who looked amazingly like the computer drawing the geeks had developed. This man was working at an advertising agency as an artist for promotions.

But when Bower talked to the agency, it seemed the man did most of his work from home. He was paid for the project, so the agency did not care how much time he spent away from the office. Had Joella helped get him out of the country and far away from this city?

The proper sub, who had served for a long time, would do anything ordered by the Dom, including taking a paid trip overseas. But Bower had to wonder if that same sub could be a killer on command.

Getting a notice from Rob that she had important information, he drove to a quiet street where he could pull up to face sideways to her van.

"So, you and the auditing forensic team have found something interesting?" Bower had stopped to get his large strong black coffee, and sipped it now as he waited for her information. If Rob was not inside working on tracing people and information, she was outside on her fancy tablet, getting in touch with those that had what she needed.

"Bower, we have been going over the membership list for the last four years. Most people are repeat associates since the club opened at that time."

"That would not be unusual." Bower sipped his energy drink. "There aren't that many places for like-minded individuals to meet and play. They would be glad for the safety of the club."

"Well, that word *safety* is what I want to talk about. Since the club opened, there have been seven of the members to meet unusual deaths, all in the last two years." Now, she held up the tablet to show him the screen.

She definitely had his attention as he put the large Styrofoam container into the cup holder next to his leg and gave her his full attention. "No one else at the club, except Prentice and the other two we are investigating, right?"

"Sure. That would have been too easy. No. Of the seven, two committed suicide, one overdosed, and one jumped off the Strafford Bridge."

Interrupting her, Bower nodded. "I remember that company executive who jumped. It was looked into and cleared."

"Hey, it gets better. There were two who were killed in auto accidents. In both cases, they were alone in their very expensive cars and were hit-and-run victims, about five months apart." Rob paused and let this sink in for a minute. "Remember the Sheriton heir who got accidentally killed in a hunting accident? He was a member."

Running the information through his head, Bower was beginning to see a pattern, but he didn't interrupt his partner.

"The last couple I have to add to our list are probably the strangest. There was Margolin, the TV reporter who got shot in a bank robbery. He was the only one inside the small branch beside the manager and a couple of tellers when it was held up by one man who fired an automatic wildly and only hit Margolin. We have never caught that bank heist guy yet."

Scrolling with a finger on her screen, she shook her head. "But that is not the weirdest death of the seven. Walter Tellman III was electrocuted on a circus ride where the wires went wrong, and the bars dropped onto the cars. Others were injured, but he was the only one killed." Now she stopped and looked between the two car windows at her handsome partner, whose movie star face hid such a brilliant mind.

"Murder for hire?" Bower mumbled as he picked up the large cup and thought this information through.

"But why?" As a well-trained detective, Rob had gone through all the physics classes and read some additional items on the strange obsessions of what looked like normal people. "They were making so much money at the club."

"Well, partner, greed is a never-ending, hungry beast. Besides, if there are partners and this is a group or gang thing, then the money is divided, and there might not be enough to go around." Now Bower was looking at the list of names on his own car computer that Rob had sent by email.

"Hell, Bower. That leaves us with seven, no eight counting Prentice, grieving but wealthy widows. After insurance payoffs and the businesses going on or settled or sold and huge properties, wow, where do we start?" Looking down at her screen that lit up her face, she began to scroll through the names.

Smiling, Bower looked up at his partner in her van. "I think we need to talk to all the grieving widows first."

As usual, finding people was not as easy as it seemed on the TV shows. People often moved. Some had Post Office Boxes instead of a living address. There were important people who preferred not to be bothered by salesmen. The seven widows were either easy to find an address or impossible to meet with personally. It all came down to the money and what they did with it after the funeral.

The easiest widow to find was Josaphine Margolin, the widow of the TV reporter. First, she had upgraded to the better side of the city into an impressive mansion and had already remarried. She was now Mrs. Garrison Patterson, who the Mr. happened to be a very young law clerk.

The partners decided that Rob would make contact with the office, and between her and the electronics group, they would get present locations of the other six widows. Bower now took his low rider over to the side of the city, where the streets were wide, well-lit, and quiet. It was the idea he would interview the Margolin/Patterson lady if she were still awake.

The house wasn't the largest in the area, but it was definitely a step up from what the TV reporter had previously. It looked like there had been more than just the usual insurance policy for the poor widow. The place was bright with lights, both outside and inside, so when the detective pulled up by the front door, he was surprised that his was the only vehicle to park in the wide driveway. This seemed to indicate that they had no visitors tonight.

The door was answered by a mature woman in a plain black dress with a small apron. Bower identified himself and asked to talk to Mrs. Patterson. He was led into a sitting room with a nice fire blazing in the large fireplace that took up most of one wall. The wait wasn't long, as he heard the approach of high heels on the floor outside the open doorway.

The widow Josaphine was in her late thirties, trying to stay young with bleached blonde hair and a pair of tight satin pants. "Well, well. The police have improved." She smiled and moved around to walk toward a settee in front of the fire. By the time she turned to sit down, she had managed to unbutton more of the purple blouse to expose her breasts. This lady was loose and on the hunt.

Not wanting to waste time playing any games with her, Bower went right to the throat. "Mrs. Patterson, what contact did you have in the past with the owners of Club La Masque?"

Now was the time for the stammering, the clearing of the throat, and the lies as she fluttered her false eyelashes. "I don't know what you mean. Rose," the lady yelled out to call the maid. "We need coffee."

That was how the conversation went—lots of interruptions, claims of not understanding, and a request for a repeat of the question. This lady was guilty of something, but the detective realized he wasn't going to get an answer from her in this lovely room.

"Lady, you have a problem. You need to appear at Precinct Thirty-Three tomorrow at six-thirty in the evening. If you don't appear, a warrant will be issued for your arrest." With that, he started for the door. Perhaps in a different setting, they could get some solid answers from her.

To his surprise, she followed him all the way to the front door, stepping out to be highlighted by the bright glow from overhead fancy lamps. As he turned his car around to leave and looked out through the open side window, he was amazed.

Raising a hand, Josaphine smiled and called out a goodbye as she waved. This woman was missing some marbles. He put in a call to his partner to run a deep detail on this woman's finances before and after her first husband's death. If there was some tie into a group that was part of the murder for hire, this flighty broad would be the one to make big mistakes in her records.

There were only two more of the widows still living in the city, so Rob and a uniform officer called on the widow of Walter Tellman III. The lady was abiding in the large mansion that she had inherited, and it was an old, prestigious place on acres of lawns. Of course, there was a large metal gate and tall bushes that separated the old home from the rest of the area.

It was announced that the lady was indisposed and not accepting visitors. After showing her credentials, Rob indicated that the lady would be expected at the precinct tomorrow for an interview, or a warrant would be issued. The lady appeared at five in the afternoon with three people from the law office that represented her. Having money was great.

But that next evening, both Rob and Bower faced three lawyers who never let the refined lady speak. When asked about her connection to La Masque club, the attorneys all protested and claimed it was only her husband's bad habits.

When presented with copies of payments and a large amount to the club after Mr. Tellman's death, the three conferred with the lady and announced they would have an answer after meeting with the accountant.

As they walked out together, Rob stared up at her handsome partner and made a comment. "Did you forget to shave today? That stubble is thick."

Shrugging, Reed nodded at his partner. "I'm going for a beard, so I have a tougher look to the street people."

"Sure." Rob smiled. "And perhaps a look not so sweet with the ladies?" Rob often wondered why the big guy had never married, with so many women throwing themselves at him.

They had a note at Bower's desk that a lady had come in to answer some questions and was in Interrogation Five. This was Mrs. Josaphine Patterson, widow of the TV reporter Margolin. She had been deposited into one of the rooms that had an attached viewing room with one-way glass. The door to the viewing room was open, and several men were standing around with coffee mugs.

When the two partners entered the main room, they both

understood all the interest and gawking. Josaphine was leaning against the table and was quite a sight. She had on heels
so high that she could only take small steps. Wearing a very
tight black skirt that was almost too short to be called a skirt.
As she sat on the edge of the table, the tight black pulled up
on one side to make everyone wonder if she wore any panties.

With her hair teased out in all types of curls, she would
have looked top-heavy if it wasn't for her large exposed
breasts. To show off those doctor-improved round globes, she
had on a bright red long-sleeve blouse with ruffles at what
would be a neckline. Except the blouse was undone almost to
the top of the black skirt.

Both detectives let out big sighs as they took seats with
their backs to the viewing window. This was going to be a
long night.

Chapter Thirteen

Never in a very long time had Reed felt so worn out after an interrogation interview. Among the offers and inuendoes the lady made constantly, there were tidbits of her dead husband's actions in the last week. And yes, they used separate banks.

She admitted she did know Mrs. Reviv. "A very nice lady who has great clothes taste." Josaphine also added, a couple of times, how helpful Mrs. Reviv had been in getting through all the paperwork connected with dear Roger's untimely death. Josaphine required a bottle of water with a lemon in it and two trips to the bathroom. To her obvious disappointment, Rob handled the bathroom trips and brought the water minus a lemon.

In the meantime, the boys behind the window got quite a view for their time. She managed to find many ways to lean, stretch, and pull to almost display her babies. It was defying gravity that kept that red blouse covering enough to allow the interview to be legal.

But later, after many had volunteered to escort the lady home, Rob and Bower listened to Josaphine's recordings and made notes when they found what they were needing. The lady dropped names and meetings with people that they knew would need to be followed and researched.

Stopping to rest their ears and the note-taking, both detectives took a minute to think over the pile of folders and notepads full of notes.

"This is stupid." Rob sat back in the closed in area of Reed's work station. "We have what looks like several possible murders for hire, and one dead guy doesn't fit."

Shifting, Reed reached over and pulled down the reporter's fat file. "What makes him different, and what does he do?"

"He's a TV reporter." Rob leaned back and looked at her partner's dark jaw as he started a successful short beard.

"No, partner." Reed had a small smile. He never produced big smiles or grins, and now, with the hairy chin, he was beginning to look a bit dangerous, handsome but dangerous. "He was an investigative reporter. He studied and researched and bothered the police to get some shocking news or information."

"Oh." A look of understanding swept over Rob's face as she grabbed her strange small laptop. "He wasn't killed because a woman wanted to be a widow. He was killed because somewhere, he found out too much."

"So, let's go talk to the people at the broadcasting station." Bower stood up and reached for his long leather coat.

It seemed that news broadcasting stations and their offices were like the police. They were called 24/7, and even in the second-floor office location for workers, about half the cubes were occupied. At the far end of the large, brightly lit room were a couple of large glass-enclosed offices. One was busy with what had been identified at the present shift's head director. As Reed got close, he saw that at one side was a stairwell that led down to the broadcast area.

Even a big, tough cop who needed a shave could not get past the man who was in charge and a couple of words — warrant and attorney. This older man was as tough as Reed and had probably gotten the top night job the hard way. He had worked his way up from the streets.

So, other than an entertaining walk through the station and

seeing its process, Reed was walking slowly to his ride while thinking of the next move. One thing he always did was be totally aware of his surroundings, even if distracted.

There was someone moving fast in his direction from the same door that Bower had exited from the broadcast station. Bower took the two final steps to his car, then turned, having his back covered by the strong, low Mustang.

The guy stopped a few paces back, and Bower decided he wasn't a mugger. It had to be a worker from inside, as he had his white dress shirt's sleeves rolled up. Bower opened his coat to make sure the man would see his detective's badge.

Looking over his shoulder, the man held out a memory stick. "I didn't give this to you. If they catch me, I'll be dead too." He waited only until Bower had the stick, then turned and went down a dark, narrow side alley. The reflection from the white shirt and the man disappeared in seconds.

Leaning back on the car, Bower pushed back his coat and put a hand into the pocket of the heavy pants. He always wore them in cooler weather and to protect him if he was down on the ground. Now, he examined the front doors that did not show anyone, and he took time to glance up at the office windows. He wanted to make sure that the exchange had not been witnessed.

There were no on-lookers above, and the street was empty, so Bower decided the man who gave him a gift was safely gone. The man in the white shirt probably went to the men's room and then went back to his job.

Getting into his ride, Bower drove slowly as he put in a call to his partner. Rob would get the memory chip into her great little computer and share with him what it contained.

Eight blocks later, through the dark back streets with plenty of people watching from doorways, Bower pulled into an empty parking lot. Rob was already there, so he pulled up beside her car, driver's window to driver's window.

"While you were at the broadcast station, I ran checks on the widows who are no longer in the city. I did pick up the extra warrants, so we can start looking at their phone and financial records." Rob reached out to receive the USB flash drive. "Wow, a customized stick, and it has MBS printed on it."

"Makeover Broadcasting Systems." Bower pointed out what the initials meant as he looked around the dark parking lot. Being a night person and a cop, he always was looking for trouble. He wanted to see something before he got a surprise. "This spot is so dirty even the druggies don't hang out here."

"Yep," Rob said as she worked with her special computer. "But there were two different murders in this lot last year."

In less than an hour, Rob reported that among several companies the reporter was investigating, one was the Club La Masque. The reporter had been chasing down ties in strange financial moves that would avoid IRS.

With that, they both separated and went on to scan the streets and help in other standard calls.

For the next two shifts, Rob chased anything available on their widows that could be found without warrants. Then, with a couple of warrants, she began to find and copy phone records and public financial information.

For Reed, his nights were full of following the people that came out of the office side door at the club. If you couldn't get a sub to kill for you, would you go out and hire a killer? In his mind, greedy people will do anything. One thing Reed had observed over his years of catching people who killed someone was that they didn't fit a mold. People were different from each other in many ways, so a *for hire killer* could be your next-door neighbor and even help with the hedge trimming.

The one man that caught Reed's attention left the club's office side door and went over to get into an SUV. It was the car that tipped Bower off as it was a plain family type SUV. It didn't shout the money that everyone else's ride shouted and parked in this side parking lot. Sure, there might be a special sub for some Master that wasn't wealthy, but they dressed good and went through the front door. They probably had been picked up in the Master's Bentley. This club was not affordable for the average customer.

Following the perceptibly standard SUV at a distance, Reed put in a call to a special desk at headquarters. He asked for a report on the license number of the vehicle he was tracking. The desktop came back with an ID with and identification on the card. The desk cop was able to give him the name of the car license owner, it was Stanley Robinson. His address was on the south end of the town and they were heading in that direction now.

Within 45 minutes, they reached a section of town that had only three and four-story buildings. Most were backed up tight together, with a brick building on the corner for groceries or bars. It was not a rundown area, it held nice buildings with a clean street.

Now, it was time to involve others, so he needed to return to the office. What he needed was a lot of information on Mr. Robinson. Walking into the busy nighttime offices, Bower was reminded that crime and criminals worked anytime but preferred the night and its hidden shadows. In Precinct Thirty-Three, there was a full staff on duty for each shift. There were a few stares on Bower as he removed his long coat and threw it over an empty chair.

"Evenin' guys." Bower nodded at the two detectives in a cube across from him.

"Hey, Bower. Do you need any help in going back inside that special club?" This was Tony, a detective who had been on the job for years. His question brought out chuckles from others in the area of this section.

"Well, Tony." Reed added a half smile. "I'll buzz you the next time I need any extra help." This also brought some snickers and low comments. "By the way, has anyone seen my partner?"

Tony's partner, standing behind their cube, answered, "Rob is over in the Geek Department."

Modern day police departments tried to keep up with the times. For this Precinct, there was a section that held busy workers reflecting the light of many flat screens. The section where talented individuals spent endless time, chasing information, logging in reports, watching street and personal cameras and sometimes, doing something that was close to illegal. Of course, it was all done in the name of the law.

From this department came a lot of reports that detectives needed, but still, everyone referred to the Network, Electronics, and Research Department as the Geek Department. Even the people who worked at those keyboards did not mind the geek name. Moving through the semi-darkness illuminated by screens and monitors, Reed saw his partner.

"Hey, Bower." Rob waved some printouts at him. "We are hip deep in your new find, Mr. Robinson. We have an address and a cell phone number."

Nodding, Bower didn't take the papers, knowing Rob would send him everything on his cell phone. "I knew his address when I followed him home. It's a nice part of the south side of the city with clean streets, and all the lamp posts lit up. His place makes him look ordinary and average."

"Yep, partner." She nodded at him and began to move to the exit of this area. "But you and I both know looks are deceiving. So, did you like the block where our man lives?"

Turning and stopping his friend with all the paperwork. "Okay, yes, he had a nice place among similar houses. It was private and secure, boxed in with the same type of places in that block." He waited, knowing Rob had something to share.

"Well, he not only owns that house but the whole block." Now, Rob raised her eyebrows, waiting to see his reaction.

Keeping his voice low as they walked around cubes with workers, he disappointed the female detective with his usual poker face. "So, does he own the house or not?"

"Sure, and he also owns the other houses beside his. In fact, he owns the whole block." Rob did smile as she saw a slight reaction behind that neat black beard.

"How does a man do that? I had him pegged at an average income job." Now Bower wondered what else his friend was going to say.

She did wave the papers again. "Well, he reported to the IRS on his tax return that he earned eighty two thousand dollars. It says he does general bookkeeping. But we traced back the ownership papers on the other houses on his block. It seems a company called MLC Corporation bought the houses. Some had liens that the Corporation paid off. There are five names in the Corporation. Of course, Stanley is one, and so is his dead grandparents, his father, and someone called Dawn Lowe. Miss Lowe is a dancer at a rough bar out on the north side of town."

"So, it's a shell company that our Mr. Robinson can hide funds and own a lot of town houses. Is his father into anything besides being connected to the company?" Reed kept his voice low but demanding.

Rob chuckled. "The poor ole dad is in a nursing home. He is stated in the records as being senile and unable to hold conversations or recognize people or things."

"Let's take this to the chief along with what we have on the widows and get more help." Reed's long legs took them to the outside hallway and down to the open door of the shift chief.

The chief was not only agreeable, but added a team from Sex Perversions Department. They investigated kidnapped females that were sold into the sex trade. They had their attention on La Masque for some time as at least three young women had disappeared from that club's location.

Now there were two top teams connected by the club and sharing information. When both teams together spent some time following information on Stanley Robinson, they found a tag to IRS agents. Upon contacting the agent, they were told that Robinson's spending did not match his income.

Being part of a team was not Bower's favorite position. He felt he worked the best on his own. It didn't take him long to slip away and slide into his car. Now, he drove past Robinson's block, and it was quiet, with most of the lights off, even in the one where he had seen Robinson enter through the garage. While he was checking on places, he drove over to the front of the Club La Masque.

CHAPTER FOURTEEN

I t, too, was dark, but large, colorful posters announcing the date of reopening were posted. Bower pulled into the side parking lot so that he could back out and return the way he had traveled. In the empty lot, his lights hit the side of the club and its private side door. His foot hit the brakes as he registered that the door was partly open. He stopped, leaving it at an angle in the middle of the area.

Shutting off the Mustang, he got out, careful not to close the door with any noise. Walking over to the dark, half-open entrance, he stopped and leaned against the outside wall. Pulling his weapon, he led with it as he slowly pushed the door to the side. It swung with no sounds to a place against the outside wall. There was no light in the hallway, but somewhere inside, there was a pale glow.

Moving slowly to make no sound, Bower crept forward using one wall as security. At the end of the short entrance hall, the choice was to go into the office where Joella ran everything, the other way led into the main room near the end of the liquor bar. His memory served him well as he now walked on carpet and looked into the office. The uncomfortable surprise was the office door was open. Joella was strict and paranoid enough to always have the door shut.

Two long steps let Bower look into the empty room with only a small office light on. That left the next choice to enter the main room. Although, even before he entered, he could tell there was a source of light off to the side. Carefully checking both sides before stepping through the door, he stopped to look behind the bar.

Feeling he was alone in this side of the large room, he made his way, gun first, to the staging areas. It was from that place the held the illumination. Using the dark around him, he was careful not to hit any furniture so that his appearance could be a surprise if anyone were in the electrical gleam from the second staging area. In the semi-dark staging section, the glow was from a spotlight aimed at the large solid X frame. This padded device was upright and tall. It was meant to restrain a sub with legs apart on the bottom portion and arms tied to the top two extensions. At the present time, it was occupied by someone constrained with head dropped down.

Making his way against walls to move around the frame to check for whoever had tied a female on the stanchion. Passing on through to the other rooms, unfortunately, Reed felt he was alone in the club except for the female in the staging area. Now, he moved up to the woman, and his first check on a pulse indicated the lady was dead. Her body was covered with bruises and slashes with blood already dried from deep wounds. Someone had done an evil deed on this corpse.

With trepidation, he lifted the head that wore the only thing on the body. It was a mask for a special sub as the wired decorations on one side moved as he lifted the chin.

Behind the mask, he was looking at the late owner of the club, Joella Margret Reviv. He went down on one heel and pulled out his phone.

By dawn, there were so many police vehicles around that the parking lot was full, and the street was blocked off in both directions.

Forensics was working hard to keep police and others from the crime scene. It was one of the strangest murders that most had ever come in contact with or seen. In blue protective booties, the coroner had pronounced the woman dead, possibly from injuries that caused blood loss. He stepped back and took off the booties that had blood on them, and placed them into an evidence bag.

Someone had whipped the bound woman on the spread X stanchion with something that cut deep into the flesh. The beautiful naked woman had died a slow, painful death. Bower thought that even the *safe word* would not have saved her. Bower's experience, as a Master and a detective, was aware that every sub had a *safe word* that was meant to stop any action immediately. The person who tied her to the platform had meant to kill her in a slow and hurtful way. Many of the deep slashes would have taken her life, But the lacerations continued in some mad desire to disfigure her and be sure she no longer was of this world. Her mouth had not been covered, so her screams would have been heard within this soundproof section.

The blood on the floor around the display scene was thick and in pools, but the scatter from the whip or whatever strange weapon had thrown blood everywhere. The high ceiling even had blood drops on the light fixtures. The person who perpetrated this evil act must have been covered in throwback splashes of Joella's life fluids. However, the extra CSI workers could not find any traces of smudges, prints, or any drops except within the special section. How did the killer leave without all kinds of traces from the gore on his or her clothes?

After waiting by his car after making the report, Bower was once again in the parking lot. Everyone who was not working directly inside had been given a job. This also included street cops, and even some other detectives had been sent to search every trash bin within walking distance. If the killer had worn a safeguarding cover or suit, he had changed or removed it by her body before leaving. For him to remove all traces of the act meant he had planned in advance and was covered from a throwback.

Thinking of the entire scene with the naked, damaged female body inside, Bower leaned on his car. He decided that whoever did this deed was too organized to throw his blood-covered clothes away in a trash bin nearby.

A detective, Russel, came out and walked over to join Reed. He got out a pack of cigarettes and lit up. He also turned and leaned on the low Mustang as he looked at the open side door of the club. "They are going through the office. The computer is gone, or just the important part, the tower." Russel pointed with his cigarette.

"My partner may help out on the computer. I will let her know, and she can meet with the Geek Squad." Bower turned and opened his car door. "I need to get out of here because I need to check on an investigation person."

Detective Russel was a help as Bower turned on the hidden police lights and began to move backward. Russel was waving people out of the way and using vehicles to back up.

Driving above the local speed limits, Bower went across town to the nice block that Robinson owned.

Although the street was well-lit by standard lamps, the houses on Robinson's side were all dark except for the front doorways and the lights on each side of the one important garage. Parking around the corner by the small corner liquor and food store, Reed went on foot. First, he used the alley behind the store and the other houses. It was wide, with small lights on some of the buildings on both sides. There were dozens of large waste bins and very little litter.

The one thing in Bower's mind as he opened his long full coat to allow easy access to his weapons. Yes, besides the thirty-three Magnum, he had a small thirty-eight on his belt and another in an ankle holster. He also had a very unusual flip knife in one pocket. Pulling out his small police flashlight, he approached a door he thought was the rear of Robinson's garage. If he could get inside the houses here, he thought the best place where there might not be full alarms was the enclosed parking area.

Examining the door carefully with the light, he could not see anything unusual about it. There was one strong lock below the doorknob, and as usual, the hinges showed the door opened out into the alley. There was no warning sign and no apparent wires. Using his knife, he checked around the edge and didn't run into a standard alarm, usually attached near the top. If it was a trip alarm when the door was opened outward, he should be able to feel the contact points.

Putting away the knife, he pulled out a small flat case and got two small tools. It took him seconds with the two utensils to get the door unlocked. There was no car parked in the garage when he quietly worked his way inside. The large area was very clean, and to his disappointment, there was nothing in this room. There were no shelves or benches and the usual work tools a person acquired with a garage. There weren't even any extra gas cans or a trash barrel.

After two hours of searching room after room, in different connected houses, he could not find anything unusual. Some of the rooms, full of furniture, were dusty from no one using them. Which room did Stanley sleep in and call his own? Nothing was evident with so many furnished bedrooms.

Moving back through the connecting doors and down to the garage, Bower realize he hadn't even found anything to use to get a judge to issue a warrant. He needed to talk to the IRS team to see if they had what might be available for more information.

Feeling he had been careful enough not to leave any trace that he had been inside, he still had a problem. He had no way to get the heavy door lock in place when he left. He had to leave it closed tightly but unlocked. Since he wore gloves and had hard sole shoes that didn't leave a print even in dust, he still knew that this intelligent man would know someone had been inside.

Chapter Fifteen

Detective Reed Bower's shift was about over, so after checking on the large police presence at the club, he called headquarters to log out. He wasted no time heading for his bed. But in the middle of a sweet dream, the chime of his cell phone woke him up. It was the Chief informing him to come in for a special meeting of the entire team.

Two hours later, Bower had worked through the same number of strong black coffees, a decision was agreed upon. The IRS investigator felt he had enough on Stanley Robinson to convict on a short term with lots of payback of funds. The plan was to involve everyone under the Government's warrant and search the five houses that filled the street that Robinson owned.

It was set up for that night. A SWAT team from their own precinct, along with another provided by the IRS investigator, was ready.

What got Bower's anger up was that he was told he was not to enter for searches but to stay with the overseer truck. Part of the reason Detective Bower was sidetracked was that he was completely against the raid. "Robinson is an intelligent killer who has been way ahead of us from the start with murders to make certain widows rich. Going into his place will gain nothing except tell him we are onto him. If we are lucky, few will be hurt by whatever traps he has set, and there is a good chance he will slip away and we will never find his new location. He has probably planned for an escape path from the time of his first kill, whoever that was."

The government agent and most of the other people involved felt Bower was off track and didn't believe law breakers were that clever. The raid was planned for the next night at1:00 am.

At 11:00 pm, a large truck with the name of Butler's Plumbing pulled in and parked a block away from Robinson's house. The driver, in a one-piece uniform with the same name on the back, got out of the driver's seat. He went to the back and opened one rear door to retrieve a large toolbox. With his load, he went up the steps of the house by the truck and went up inside. Someone had a water leak late in the night, and Butler's Plumbing advertised 24/7 service. The small statement was painted on the side of the truck.

Seven people were inside the box at the end of the truck, which was full of electronic equipment. Some were sitting, and others leaned against busy counters.

Detective Bower was sitting sideways to a radio connection, his thermos full of black coffee. The crowded area also included Bower's Chief, leaning by the camera screens. With him was the IRS agent, and shifting around were two top SWAT officers. One for the IRS teams and the other for the local police. There were a couple of lightweight, portable AC units to keep the electronics cool. Still, Reed felt the air was stale and beginning to smell of people.

Out on the streets, the first few officers were slowly moving around. They were checking for citizens in the wrong places and slowly moving in the alley and up the block. Two guys in a convertible with the top down went past, the later returned to leave the area. They were plain-clothes cops. In fact, all the people who were slowly moving past the houses and across the street were cops.

Slowly, different people went into the houses across the street from Robinson's row. At one place, a man in raggedy clothes sat down on the steps. This was a try to set up safety to prevent any person rushing out to see the action. At one o'clock, there could be heard the thrum of heavy trucks. It was the SWAT armored trucks, two in front of the houses and two in the back alley.

Watching on cameras that had been placed around the block and alley yesterday, Bower saw the heavily armored people of these special teams, pour out and move in well trained squads. The idea was to hit each residence from both the front and the back. They moved so fast that it was only moments before the reports started coming in on the speakers in the truck.

What Bower was hearing at first was the short, clipped tones of the individuals as they began to make sure each room was safe and without people.

"Cleared," a man announced, and even as the same word came in over and over, there was a red light that came on a particular screen which was tracing many of the officers that wore the tags. There had been an early report from the undercover cops following Robinson that he was located at a fancy bar on the far north side. After forty-five minutes, the decision was made that all five buildings were empty. Now, the teams could slow down and begin to search for computers, paperwork, and possible items of interest.

The next hour was boring for Detective Bower as the reports kept coming in of nothing. So far, the legal invaders had not found anything.

Once, a frustrated voice came over a speaker. "Are we sure the perp even lives here?"

The IRS agent got on the communications mic and told everyone to keep comments to a minimum and keep looking harder. He was moving around behind the guys seated, and it was obvious he wished he were inside one of the houses along with his teammates.

"What about the main house?" The agent used a mic that probably went to all the teams.

"Bedroom is so neat it looks like it is never used, except for a pair of pants over a chair."

Now, another official searcher announced. "Nice SUV in the garage with keys hanging on the wall. We will look it over." This man was talking as he worked around the garage.

Suddenly, Bower sat up as the man had his attention. He picked up a mic and reached the team in the garage. "Wait, don't open the car doors. Is the thing unlocked?"

"Sure, but even if it isn't, the keys are right out in plain sight hanging on a wall." There was the sound of a second man behind the one who answered. There was also the sound of a car door opening. Suddenly, there was a car alarm.

"We need the key to shut off the alarm." This was someone talking and being picked up by mics.

Suddenly, Bower put together a plot that he knew meant death. He jumped, grabbed the other speaker of the agent, and yelled, "Get out of there. It's a trap."

He shoved the Chief and a couple of others as he struggled to get out of the truck. Someone placed a hand on his shoulder to stop him, but he yelled as he pushed out the back door. "The place is a trap, and we need to get the teams out of there."

He made it through the small, busy work area and opened one of the back doors when the truck was rocked by an ear-bursting explosion. Being the first one out of the truck didn't mean that anyone else waited. The Chief and the Agent were stumbling out right behind him. Someone inside the truck was yelling through the mics one word. "Evacuate."

Looking down the street, Bower saw a scene straight out of war. The inside of each building had erupted with flames, and all the windows and some doors were blown out to cover the street. Stanley Robinson had made sure that every building went up at the same time.

Some of the men who still had not gone into the buildings received wounds even with their special uniforms and armor. A couple of officers jumped from windows to escape. One man was dragging someone else through a blown-open door. There were injured officers who had started to rise from where the blasts had knocked them down on the street and sidewalks. Unfortunately, there were bodies that did not move.

Behind him, as he judged the damage, the Chief was waving some of the extra police forward, and the one ambulance that had accompanied as part of the original plan. Calls were being in for the fire department and additional ambulances. But due to the fact that the series of blasts was immense, the time it took for help to show up, most of the houses would be engulfed or falling inward.

It took until morning to get a count on the police that were assigned to this raid. There were already seven in some hospitals, and many more were getting minor problems patched by a couple of large open rescue trucks. But there were eleven officers either dead or still missing. It was the largest tragedy that had hit this city, and it was worse since it involved trained law officials.

But Bower had left with the sparks still floating down from the fires. He had his gun out and marched away down the middle of the street to get a ride to his car. He felt the heat of another explosion blast behind him, and more glowing particles were everywhere.

There was only one thing on the big detective's mind, and it was finding Stanley Robinson. Tired and angry, Bower thanked a cop who had provided a ride to his car. After getting up the evening before, he had spent the full night with the chaos at the block that was on fire. But his adrenalin was still high in his body, and he drove slowly, approaching the south side.

Over the cop radio, someone spoke to all available law officers, whether in vehicles or on the beat.

"Need security check on police officer not responding." This was followed by a street address, and Bower immediately turned his car around in the middle of a street. He responded over the inside radio mic, indicating he was handling the call. The address had been for the La Masque club.

Choosing first to slowly drive by the dark club with crime scene tape still attached, he saw nothing. But that was a real problem since a policeman had been posted to stay in front to stop sightseers. The parking lot and even the street were empty. But in the morning light, he saw an expensive Lexus parked to the curb. There were no other cars until he reached the second intersection and returned. He parked across from the Lexus, and with a gun in his hand and his long coat open, he approached the parking area first.

Intending to go in through the private side door, it had yellow tape across it and a clumsy, simple outside lock that had recently been added. Stopping and pulling out a closed knife that he was able to flip open, he thought that the policeman, whether alive or not, had to be inside the front door that was not locked. The thick blade easily snapped off one part of the simple screwed-on lock. Now, the detective entered slowly, checking the short hall with the daylight behind and no lights on inside.

After being here so many times, he was aware that the club was meant to be dark, with small lights in a few areas and movable bright lights for demonstrations. There was a soft reflection from light in the main scenario area. Bower was glad to move into the shadows by the bar. He felt better as he was no longer outlined by the sunlight in the back hallway. Moving behind the bar, leading with his gun, he came out at the point that led into the display section.

Leaning against the wall, which was the darkest area in the room, he slid forward until he had a complete view of the large X display area. There, he saw a sight that was comparable to when the club was in full action. The trim, unconscious, naked man tied to the cross looked dead. There was no movement to his body, no chest rising, and his head hung down. By the short military haircut, Bower guessed that this was the missing policeman.

Standing off to one side was a man dressed as a Dom. That meant he had on boots, a tight pair of pants low on his hips, and nothing else. He had something in his hand that Bower couldn't recognize at this distance. But even this far away, Detective Bower knew he had found the killer. Stanley Robinson was moving toward the tables.

Before stepping forward, Bower hit the emergency button on his cell phone, which was in his front shirt pocket.

"Need back up at La Masque club. Officer down." He spoke quietly but in a firm voice and watched as Robinson turned toward him. That was when he saw what was in the killer's hands. In one, he held a special mask that was expensive and used by male Doms. In the other, he had a small pistol.

Chapter Sixteen

This was going to be a standoff as Bower walked forward with his gun out in the two-handed grip. Stanley jerked around and brought up the gun hand.

"Drop the gun," Bower growled. "You are under arrest."

With a quick step, Stanley moved over to the side of the trussed-up policeman's body.

"Ah." Robinson seemed to sigh. "The famous Detective Bower. Of course, it would be you that has approached me."

"Mr. Robinson, I mean what I say. Put down the gun. Let's make this reasonable."

"Oh, detective. Our lives are not reasonable." Robinson waved the gun as he spoke.

"You have a mask?" Reed asked the obvious question.

Now Robinson also held up the special black mask with gold beads draped across it. "I'm not stupid. If your people found it hooked behind the scene prop, they would have found my DNA. So, I needed to claim it before someone did ask why it was still here."

Moving slowly forward, Bower did have to wonder why the CSI team had missed a mask when they collected evidence in this room. There had been several masks that were now held in storage at the Precinct, along with a lot of other interesting items.

In this dark, soundproofed room, Bower couldn't hear any sounds from outside, but he knew that there were many police on their way to answer the call, *officer down*. For right now, he was facing a killer that he wanted to, no, needed to stop.

"You're not getting out of here alive. Drop the gun, and let's end this." Now Bower spoke louder and firmer as he watched the other man closely. He was aware that the other man was still pointing the gun at him. He was trying to decide how to get the upper hand or distract Robinson. He was saved by the thumping at the far away front door. The backup had arrived.

With the noise, Stanley jerked backward and fired the weapon. Bower made a dive to the floor, seeking any cover as he felt the pain in his left arm. He had been hit. Ignoring the pain and shock of the wound, he rolled sideways and fired upward at Stanley's chest. The big Magnum bullet knocked Robinson backward as the man fired off one more shot that went wild.

Four hours later, sitting on the edge of the back of an ambulance, Bower was given the news. The wanted killer, Mr. Stanley Robinson, was dead. Bower was told he was found at no fault in the situation. Unfortunately, he had to give up his weapon to CSI, and he was on paid leave for six days until a full review was recorded. Personally, he felt he could sleep for six days, so nothing was lost.

It was only midnight that Detective Reed Bower was awakened by a call from headquarters. He was back on duty with a clear shoot on his record. More important, there was a murder that he should handle immediately. There was a body hanging by his neck on the outside of a second-story window. He had been shot before the hanging. He was the owner of a strip nightclub. He also was the late husband of Rose Stellar. She was the previous widow of Dr. Frank Stellar, who had been killed at the sex Club La Masque.

With a sigh, Bower checked out his large Magnum and put on his long leather coat. Work called.

The End

About the Author

M. Garnet, author of over 80 novels, is known by her friends and fans as Muriel Garnet Yantiss, so you will find her on Facebook under that name. But her website is under her author's name, aNET.M. Garnet has written for many years and has many books on a cross-genre, but all seem to be Happy Ever After.

Her own long and exciting life adds details to her stories that bring a complete and interesting process that gives the reader some education that they might not have known about before reading her books. The inside workings of foundries, the fact of diamond mining on Inuit territory in Canada, and best of all that, we already found a way to talk instantly from point to point to break Einstein's theory on Faster than Light.

As an active member of the local chapter of Florida West Coast Writers and was the 2019 Book Challenge Coordinator for the group. She has been a long-time member of the NAPW and has done presentations and short articles for years. M. Garnet enjoys her membership in Science Fiction & Fantasy Writers of America.

Her writing has won her many awards and reviews. These include the 2017 Golden Heart, 2017 Rita, 2016 Sexy Scribbles, 2016 Passionate Ink, 2016 Shelf Best Indie Book, 2015 National Novel Writing Month Winner, along with top reviews on many of her Novels.

Ain't life grand?

Drop Muriel a note, she loves to hear from people and

answers everyone. mgarnet2@yahoo.com

Don't forget to add a review where you got this story, as it helps others and the author.